Clinical, Brutal...

An Anthology of Writing with Guts

Clinical, Brutal...
An Anthology of Writing with Guts

Edited by Christopher Nosnibor

2010
Clinicality Press
York, England

Clinical, Brutal... An Anthology of Writing with Guts
This collection Copyright © 2010
Copyright remains the property of the respective authors.

First published in 2010 by Clinicality Press, York
http://clinicalitypress.co.uk

ISBN 978-0-9556939-2-2

Contents

Introduction

Cut to the Quick: A Brief History of Clinical Brutality

Christopher Nosnibor

At some point in 1998 or 1999, I was working on a novel that's still languishing unpublished and had just written the section which later became 'Solitary Brother,' which appeared (somewhat belatedly) in issue 2 of *Paraphilia Magazine*. I wasn't in the best frame of mind when I wrote it. I was pissed off with life, with the world and its inhabitants, and I found some small relief in venting my anger in fantasy. Sort of. I was also discovering – even then – that it's difficult to get noticed in an increasingly overpopulated, media-saturated postmodern world, and that while it's evermore difficult to evoke shock in a desensitised audience, extremity is generally a reliable means of drawing attention to oneself.

The trouble with shock is that it has limited currency, its effects short-lived, even if it is exercised as a means to an end and there's a genuine point to or behind itit. The failing of so much extremity is that it soon wears, and that so much of is thin, blatant, obvious, po-faced and puerile. Schlock, horror... yawn. So while shock has its merits and its functions, innovation is where it's really at if you want to stand out from the crowd. From this came an idea: I thought it would be hilarious and novel to combine extreme violence with medical terminology. It couldn't fail, being the perfect blend of shock and innovation. I began writing with a copy of *Gray's Anatomy* to hand in order to provide that 'technical' – or 'clinical' – aspect to some fairly brutal scenes. With a couple of friends, I devised the concept of 'clinical brutality' – those everyday acts of violence recounted crisply, factually and using technical rather than literary flourishes.

In retrospect, it was reading Stewart Home's novel *Slow Death* that sowed an early seed for the concept: the countless references to 'liquid DNA' and the like were striking, as absurd as they were amusing, and yet, at the same time, it made perfect, albeit warped, sense. But as with most influences, this became absorbed into an evolving perspective along with myriad other elements, and all on a subconscious level.

Being young and naive, we thought we could change the face of literature. We wanted to be the next Beat Generation. Or something. We got excited. We wrote lots and exchanged ideas and pieces of hastily-typed stories that never would each completion.

We set up a website to showcase our work and called it 'Clinicality' to reflect the new genre, as well as our desire to revolutionise publishing. These were very different times: the Internet simply wasn't the immense medium it is now. There was a mirror site, too: Columbiannecktie.org.uk. I'd been listening to Big Black a lot at the time, and Albini's approach to both subject matter and production could be described as brutal, if not necessarily clinical. Whatever. Both got shut down after a matter of just a few months (probably because we included stolen images of blood-spattered corpses and famous corporate logos, although it's equally likely that it was simply because they were free domains and we didn't maintain them and they received practically zero traffic).

Meanwhile, I completed work on *Exiled in Domestic Life*, and submitted it, as well as various short stories, to countless publishers and accumulated an impressive collection of rejections in the process. Many publishers didn't even bother to reject my offerings. Over time, I came to realise that the trouble with being innovative was that convincing people who operate in business terms of its merits and marketability was, to put it mildly, extremely difficult. It was ever thus: the avant-garde has long broken new ground, its innovative exponents existing in the shadows on the peripheries while their ideas are subject to dilution and eventual acceptance and mainstream absorption and some other fucker gets rich and famous on the back of it. Like the Murphy's, I'm not bitter. I just wanted to make that vital breakthrough, for the innovation that was clinical brutality to exist in the public domain and perhaps be subject to dilution and eventual mainstream absorption in a more marketable, palatable form.

Time passed. The breakthrough never came. I lost touch with my collaborators, but the idea endured, and I incorporated clinical brutality in a number of pieces through the years. Most remains unpublished at the present time, although 'Party Hard' which appears in *Bad Houses* features some key elements of the style, and I'm rather pleased to have succeeded in excavating one or two pieces – of mine and others – which I had presumed lost for inclusion here. I believe they still hold up pretty well.

Anyway, time and technologies change and a couple of years ago I learned that it was possible to publish a book without needing any money or contacts whatsoever, and it was even possible to do this and have instant access to a global market. It was around this time that I also discovered social networking, and through MySpace came into contact with a lot of writers who were producing work that was far more exciting than the majority of stuff that was being published conventionally. What's more, I found myself coming into contact with authors who, in various ways, broadly demonstrated elements that fitted into the 'clinical brutality' framework. Perhaps 'my' innovation wasn't entirely mine – perhaps it never had been – but it felt like there was a genuine creative current, a spirit that connected a disparate array of powerful and unique literary voices. I began to get excited all over again.

I had continued to send stuff to publishers sporadically during the intervening years, but my approaches were invariably met with general disinterest, and while frustrating, it dawned on me that the disinterest was mutual. Most of the publishers weren't – and still aren't – putting out anything remotely risky or even interesting, and certainly nothing that struck me as being remarkably innovative. Either that, or their scopes were, and remain, so narrow and prescriptive you have to wonder who they're trying to please other than themselves. And so it came to pass that I decided to do something about it, and to revive the 'Clinicality' idea with the assistance of longstanding f(r)iend Stewart Bateman. The timing felt right. This was the post-*C.S.I.* generation, after all. Perhaps the world was at last ready. Thus, Clinicality Press was born.

The book you are holding requires little further explanation in real terms. The works contained herein combine to summarise the Clinicality aesthetic. It's by no means exhaustive, of course, and isn't intended to be definitive. *Clinical, Brutal* is intended as a taster, and as a means of demonstrating how the concept of Clinical Brutality can manifest itself in many divers ways. However, all of the works contained herein share a passion, a power, and an unswerving commitment to showing life the way it really is. Clinical Brutality isn't a movement, nor is it a genre or style. It's a perspective, an approach, and one that demands fearlessness from both the writer and reader. It's clinical, brutal, cutting edge. Excessive gore is not a prerequisite, but nor is it frowned upon. It's all about those small, everyday random acts of violence, not all of which are physical or even necessarily entirely tangible, that are common to us all. Those little psychological pains we inflict on one another, the words that resonate long after they've cut deep, the behaviours we exhibit that make others uncomfortable or act in a certain way because we seek to manipulate a situation or an individual, or sometimes simply because we're pissed off or because we can... those are equally brutal, and so often clinical in their calculated execution. It's strange to think that humanity seems to consider itself to be the very apogee of evolution given these behaviours that are common to us all, every single day.

It's impossible to overstate just how delighted I am to be presenting so many authors, every one of whom I greatly respect and admire and who, above all, excite me, in one place: rare, unique talents and remarkably powerful voices, one and all, without exception. There isn't the space here to go into each of the authors who have contributed to this book. Moreover, there really isn't the need. Their works speak for themselves, and require no sales pitch or recommendation from me. Writing with bite is what it's all about. Every single piece in here has just that, in abundance.

From the short observational poems that draw the most microcosmic of vignettes, to the more expansive prose pieces, all of the authors gathered here portray life in keenly-observed and painful detail, expressing it in the most unflinching and intrepid terms. Literary flourishes are kept to a bare minimum: instead, you will find stark, direct and abrasive forms, exposing the harsh realities in the brightest and whitest of lights. Every single piece stands alone as a short, sharp shock, a blade into the sagging belly of the establishment. Collectively.... this book is nothing short of explosive. Careful, it might just go off in your hands.

Enjoy!

Christopher Nosnibor, York, December 2009

Clinical, Brutal....

Blood On The Tracks

Pablo Vision

I slide up the reverb on tracks 10 through to 20 – with a bit of luck no one will be able to decipher the juvenilia that these pretty boys think so profound. Fuck, maybe I should tell them the entire thing should be backwards – Christ they're backwards enough not to realise how passé this would be. I could tell them that it would resonate in the clits of gothic pussy everywhere.

But the reverb seems to make the fucking dreadful lyrics stand out more – maybe I should plug in a series of ring modulators – render the entire thing white noise.

Moments consumed and the future derived / from a system of virtue and pleasure denied / hours devour and reason destroyed / transient moments of treasure enjoyed

Fuck knows what day the music died, but these fuckers are revelling in necrophilia; shagging its rotted corpse with pubescent cocks, and ignorant tongues.

"Yes boys, poetry indeed, how about a fucking limerick for the next masterpiece. You do realise that Spinal Tap is a fucking joke?" I do not say.

"Mint. Fucking Mint," I say. "This is going to be on Classic Albums in ten years time. Fucking Mint."

Fucking hell. All I ever wanted was to be doing this. All of my fucking life. And it is shit: an endless procession of pretty boys and girls paying homage to their heroes in their own inadequate ways. The fuckers don't even manage to find novel ways in which to express their inarticulacy – a fucking Xerox machine would be more creative.

But that is not the worst of it. The worst is seeing people – people that you have worshipped because they have got the rarest of gifts – artists who are artists rather than fame seeking delusionals – artists who mainline straight to the vein better than the finest uncut – artists who leave you unable to string together any kind of sense of what you have just experienced – artists who's piss is worth more than the entire top one hundred put together – golden, yellow, bloodstained, or otherwise – the worst is seeing these people come in and find they are no better in the flesh than the tossers I am producing now. Give them a glimpse of hard currency and they'll record fucking advert jingles, or duet with some big-titted soap-star, or just tell you they have found god (not that that is difficult with the fucking stockpiles of cut-to-size fuckers there are to choose from). Yeah, I'm cynical, but when everybody you ever put faith in lets you down without exception, you'd have to have some screwed-up vision not to see it otherwise.

So on to another piece for another track. These fuckers can't just play anything through in one go. Just bits here and there that I have to synch and pitch-shift to make something on which my reputation will depend. Thank you so very fucking much, cocksuckers.

Clinical, Brutal....

The day betrays what darkness steals / desperate subway nights conceal / city streets where strangers roam / they hunt in packs and watch unknown / the darkness which the shadows served / midnight madness dreams observed

Fucking brilliant. No one is ever going to think The Doors. No one is ever going to wonder how much progress has been made in thirty years. No one's going to think they write this shit because their cocks are so shrivelled up with speed that they are to punk too fuck. Christ don't they have virgins blood to drink, or skateboards to paint? Don't they have to be home for tea?

I have to play the keyboard part myself, because he can't get it right even after take 56, and because I can correct the notes that don't belong in this, or in any piece. I am tempted to play some Manilow melody backwards over it just so I can express my assessment of their worth.

Now Rick has got an idea. He wants to be sucked off whilst he is singing. These guys! Where do they get their ideas? It's a fucking disaster, but its over pretty quick, and some girl of fourteen has tasted the milk of human kindness on a day she will remember for the rest of her life. Now Brian wants me to mic up this other girl's cunt, whilst he eats her out, whilst she sits on the woofer. I try saying that I am not going to be able to pick anything over the bass rumble, but this isn't about making music, this is about them making history with older bits of mythology. It's as vacuous as any religion, but it is, at least, a distraction from the fucking music.

And now Brian is inspired by the muse of teenage pussy; he scribbles on a bit of paper:

He paints the violence of the sun / transcribes the moment lovers come / the overwhelming crimson skies / on canvas stretched before her eyes / and of the message there which read / 'tonight we walk amongst the dead'

Oh yes Brian, Baudelaire is using his Brian-Iblis-shaped dildo on himself right this very moment. Sixties acidhead poets are issuing writs about the first line. Why don't you go the whole hog, and kill the fucking girl. No. Instead, he makes me type out the fucking words, lest he forget, and gives the scrap of paper to the girl. A touching love token that she can treasure into her dotage.

They call it a day, and with any luck it will be weeks before they feel inclined to actually play any instruments. I am sure that there are clubs and TV shows where their presence is more urgently needed.

You don't like me? A bit bitter? Unrelenting? Try living my life, and see how you would feel. But like I say, as much as I despise creeps like these, it is the destruction of my own delusions that damage me the most. Maybe I am in an extra vitriolic mood because tomorrow I get to meet my hero. Surprise you that I have heroes? Well you don't get to hate humanity without first loving it. Why the fuck-else do you think that this is the only work I have ever wanted to do? I just wanted to serve the gods in any small way that I could, even at the sacrifice of having to twiddle knobs for cunts like Satanic Afterbirth Death

Explosion, or ProMETHeus. Every other fucker has let me down, so why should this be any different? Every other fucker has dismantled the world I choose to live in brick by brick, or with nuclear devastation, or just with the predictability of the reality. So tomorrow is the moment I have waited all my life for, and it has every probability of being yet another nail in my coffin. Maybe it will be this day; maybe it will be another day. But one day, sooner or later, as sure as we all turn to dust, he will sell-out. They all do, one way or another, they all do.

***

When he walks in it is already different. He has not brought loads of equipment. I have not received a list of things I cannot say or do in his presence. He is not stoned or drunk. There is no entourage of thousands. There are no girls with Red Snappers wriggling in their cunts. And he does not speak about anything other than what he wants: just acoustic guitar, and vocals, and just the flat acoustics of the studio.

I sit behind the desk and think that the fucker is going to start singing about gnomes or recycling, or want 500 tracks layered on top of it. I sit and I listen. And I cry. I fucking cry my heart out. And not only do I not care – I would be powerless to do anything other.

There is something in the voice that is like Nick Drake's Black Eyed Dog, or like that one small bit where Tim Hardin sings 'but will we see each other again? Oh... I hope so', but it is not either of these things. The effect is similar, but it is unique. The effect of that naked, and painfully honest voice, sends shivers down my spine, and raises goose bumps all over my body; it stops all rational thought.

I walk out from the booth and I shoot him point-blank range in the head. I go back in the booth and play the track back, again and again.

We all choose our own gods. And this god will never let me down.

Never.

Clinical, Brutal....

My Last Photograph

Inspired by the phrase 'A picture paints a thousand words'

Kestra Fay

This is my picture... that is to say, I am the subject within the photograph. Pixels, hues, an impeccable combination of shading and of highlights. Clearly, somebody was concentrating intently for that brief snap-shot of time, to capture that image of my pristine form – naked, how strange: I am normally shy – where I lay, twisted and floating in a storm of furniture and tangle of household accessories. The flotsam and jetsam of my life you could say. My pale skin gleams, beautiful hair curled and shining. Everything in perfect focus, the shutter-speed and aperture aligned just so. Depth of field is faultless, nothing is missed. The flash must have been tilted upwards, and away, to avoid the otherwise inevitable glare from the indoor scene.

Confused. Who would take the time to see that this image, of *me*, exists? I am not famous. Nor successful. Undeserving of such attention. Pondering awhile, the picture fades, developing a haze, shifting somewhat during the meditation. A chill approaches, on tip-toes, creeping gradually into being. The spell splinters. Fracturing the view, refocusing my picture. Look again. Please.

The same gentle shading blending into highlights. Pixels, hues, the perfect marriage of aperture and shutter-speed. My previously pristine form becomes something else... oh my... naked, yes. Pristine, no. My body, my broken, punctured body stares up from the picture with eyes deadened by more than mere photography. I am discarded, with the overturned furnishings. No further use for me. A sheen of brown tinged red, coating my form like a gauze. Pooled on the carpet beneath me, and drawn up into cushions around me. Dark red, verging on black, so dark.

And then: I remember. I know: I am dead, and *that* is my dead body, there in the picture. Murdered. No need to question. The last photograph, taken of me, to be used in court. Evidence for a trial. The reason for the focus, the attention to detail.

Now I drift. I have no hands to hold a photograph, no eyes to gaze upon a picture, no brain to contemplate self-pity or even revenge. I am pure energy now, I have let go of my history. A last pulse of spirit, a flickering appreciation for the man behind the lens. For the one that took my picture so well. Justice will be served, he has made sure I am not forgotten.

Clinical, Brutal....

Rubber-Hose Real-Estate

Jim Lopez

Albert Camus gave a lecture in December 1957, entitled "Create Dangerously." Camus describes Stepan Trofimovich, a character in Dostoevsky's "The Possessed," as a man who insists on being a living reproach, suffering from attacks of patriotic melancholy. It seems reasonable to say that patriotic melancholy is a thoughtless sadness enmeshed in one's loyalty to one's country; it is an inner rant that burrows deep into the mind's den, waiting to be abstracted and raised up as a symbol, the way a weary rodent is dug out of his comfortable slumber on Groundhog's Day and raised as an effigy to a bunch of lunatics, who think he is a cuddly, delightful fellow, regardless of how disturbed he may appear among the dim circumstances in a late winter day.

The American Public's concept of patriotism is packaged and sold in a McDonald's Happy Meal. It is nearly impossible to gather an effective courage to create one's own belief with loyalty to self, country, family, friends or God. "To create today is to create dangerously." Camus said of his time, "Any publication is an act, and that act exposes one to the passions of an age that forgives nothing."

Camus spoke at the height of the commercial age, which wallowed in a paradise of persuasive innocence; whereas, today commercialism has reached its period of Alzheimer's and is set in auto drive, benefiting from the hard work of Woodrow Wilson's Committee for Public Information. Forgiveness is not necessary since most of us have lost the ability to remember what we need forgiveness for and have never bent a knee in the arduous task of recollection. What is printed, published, distributed and marketed today is forgotten tomorrow, therefore, it is reasonable that time forgives nothing, because it's fading memory forgot the necessity for forgiveness. The artist's faith in him or herself has been substituted with inflated profits reaped from a successful marketing campaign.

"The most misrepresented value today is certainly the value of liberty." Camus describes how a society that was built by an elite merchant class usurped art by using "…an ideal liberty, as often as it could, to justify a very real oppression. As a result, is there anything surprising in the fact that such a society asked art to be, not an instrument of liberation, but an inconsequential exercise and a mere entertainment." In other words, art is commissioned by the ruling class to either entertain – so as to divert attention away from oppression – or art is commanded to make oppression look beautiful and sublime.

If the cradle of Western Civilization was conceived in the Fertile Crescent that spans from the Persian Gulf of Mesopotamia to Egypt's Nile River, and one man stood at its apex, why has it been difficult for the public to believe that Alexander the Great established large opium crops throughout his Empire, and that every Empire since then, to the current Empire, has vied for control over Alexander the Great's narcotics? Why is that unbelievable? The Yale graduates who went to Berlin to study Hegelian philosophy, known as the Russell Brothers, started an opium import business after the Civil War. Opium was a legitimate business that the Brits were ruling at the time and struggling with France for control over in Indo China.

So we have junkies lurking in every Empire that has ever existed, and we have junkies here in the United States, and they are supplied by legitimate merchants, such as the CIA, Pharmaceutical Corporations and Organized Crime Syndicates. And who really gives a shit? Business is business, right?

For the first time since Alexander the Great, in the 1970's, another crop of drugs rivaled opium: the South American cocaine fields. And who controls them? It takes a mere rudimentary business sense to figure it out. You don't let illegitimate business men control one of the most lucrative ventures in economic history. United States politicians and businessmen control the heroin and cocaine in the world and they wage war against any country that tries to take it away from them, as long as they don't have nuclear weapons.

A man named Addison in an article in the Princeton Review, dated 1848, Article III — Dueling — Code of Honor, (by an unknown author), is quoted: "courage is that heroic spirit inspired by the conviction that our cause is in its prosecution... When courage is calm, rational, firm, mild and just, all good men respect it and do most reverent obeisance to it."

But can courage shake the look of the raven's eye that dodges in and out of traffic, pecking at a dead squirrel that has been crushed by a garbage truck in the early morning? A person walks to work, grappling with the concept of courage, feeling as if he or she is in Aceldama, and believes they will never acquire an authentic opportunity to discover if he or she has any courage: to test one's capacity for courage.

Waightstill Avery's brave hold of his ground as a young Andrew Jackson took a shot at him, and missed, did not boil Avery's blood. Instead of taking his shot at the not yet President, Avery walked across the field and administered a lecture to Jackson, where both seconds listened attentively and called the matter settled with no blood shed. Avery's gracious stride and merciful lecture made little impact on Jackson who many years latter killed Charles Dickenson in a duel.

Avery proved himself to be a man who was not afraid to be shot at. His courage especially roared if he escaped without a wound, manifesting itself in a frightening homily of the asinine engagement of Dueling and the poor character it breeds.

A lawyer by the name of High M. Stokes, the son of General Mumford Stokes of Wilkes, challenged Samuel P. Carson of North Carolina to a gentleman's duel. Carson declined, reasoning that Stokes was no gentlemen but an indulgent drunkard. Carson had been in a gentleman's duel before with a Dr. Robert Brank Vance. This duel was on the Greenville Turnpike on the border of North and South Carolina. Vance had insulted Carson's father, slandering him a coward for not fighting the Brits during the Revolutionary War. The duel resulted in the death of Vance, while Carson went on to serve as Secretary of State in President David G. Burnett's cabinet. But Carson died an unmarried man and was said to have carried a great grief within himself for the rest of his life for killing Vance, who, while dying in his bed from the fatal wound incurred by Carson's ball shot said, "I harbor no ill will towards Carson."

Both Carson and Aaron Burr attempted to speak with their challengers after having shot them, but both Carson and Burr were rushed away by their seconds and were never permitted to speak with the dying Vance or the lion hearted Federalist, Hamilton again. Carson and Burr carried a courageous burden that few gentlemen who engage in unseemly acts will ever carry.

**

Clinical, Brutal....

I gently held Angie's wrist while she tied a lavender, paisley neck tie around her upper arm, slapping and waiting for a vein to emerge. Our eyes never left each other's, and when that vein bulged she found my soul with her gaze...then I stuck that needle in, soft and slow, pressing the plunger full of Mexican Mud into her irises.

Tino sat on the lid of his toilet while Lucy jabbed him with a speedball right in the neck.

Tino had asked me if I knew a girl who would mainline him in the jugular while he sat on the toilet in his office that was stacked wall to wall with books. He wanted me to photograph it, so there might remain some sort of a death mask of him.

Was Tino going out of his mind? I had read that between 1981 and 1985, death from speedballs had risen by 754%, and I wondered if Tino was creating courageously, or if he would end up another statistic. I knew two girls who might want to stick him in the neck – especially if he paid for their narcotics – but I'd have to go back to the neighborhood I grew up in to find Lucy and Angie.

Lucy was named after her mother's favorite Beatles' song, and Angie's father had nick-named her after his favorite Stones' song. Lucy and Angie were born at the height of commercialization's artistic expression spawning Rock-n-Roll's adolescents.

I jumped off the bus and walked down New Ave. in South San Gabriel with Chacho, a childhood friend. I hadn't seen him in fifteen years or so and was surprised he wasn't in prison or dead.

Chacho was a spindly Mexican transvestite. He looked like a mal-nourished werewolf with blood-shot eyes and cracked lips and hard taste buds that were so dried out his tongue looked like rotted wood. Chacho started jittering and scratching, and his repetitive speech was beginning to annoy me as the neighborhood sweltered like the dried desert buried under the concrete of East Los Angeles. Chacho had been on a runner, low riding around town. I asked him if he knew where Lucy and Angie were.

"They're probably at Soto's."

I picked up my pace, and made my way to the old street that embodied my childhood memories, Ramona Boulevard.

As I walked onto Soto's porch I overheard him talking to Danny, a junkie *pachuco*, who came from a long line of junkie *pachucos*.

"Where did you get the little girl?" Soto asked Danny.

"I'm telling you I murdered a junkie, and you're asking me about a *chavala* I rescued from of a demon."

A man bleeding from his ears, looking pale and stunned walked by Soto's house. I thought he was an undercover cop posing as a drug addict, but he wasn't posing.

"There goes that mother-fuckin' narc. Who the fuck's on my porch?" Soto shouted.

"I'd like to order a Fiesta-Bitch-Taco and a cup of Mrs. McGillicudy's Cunt-Bustin' Juice," I answered.

"Mother-fuckin' Jack-off!" Soto exclaimed as he walked out and grabbed me. "Dude. What-the-fuck? How long has it been, mother-fucker?"

Before I could answer Soto was yelling at the junkie walking by. "Get the fuck out of here, you low-life narc! I got nothin' for you!"

"He said your name, *hommie*, only I heard it not so much out loud, but like he whispered it into my mind," Danny said with a thick cholo accent from inside the house.

The junkie-narc turned around and started walking in a confused circle. Danny sensed this and goose bumps popped all over his body. A tingling sensation vibrated his face.

Soto walked up to the junkie-narc, and checked him out.

I poked my head through the door frame and saw Danny swaying on his feet. Danny was mumbling that he could feel his feet lifting off the floor. Then he levitated. He floated to the ceiling; the back of his neck pressed to it.

He cried out, "Soto! Soto! Pull me down, *hommie!*"

Soto handed a piece of paper to the junkie-narc, admonishing him, "You can't hackie-sack a turd you little-bitch-bone-monkey. Now fuck-off." Then he calmly walked into the house. "What-the-fuck!" Soto seized Danny's dangling arm and yanked his light body down from the ceiling. Danny's brown skin turned white. His eyes sunk deep into their pockets. He clung to Soto and in a hurried, soft voice he said, "Listen, *ese,* before it's too late. Last night in the early hour of morning my dogs were spooked by something outside, *ese.* I walked out and heard a noise I never heard before. It sounded like some kind of demonic animal. I saw a red bull across the street on my neighbor's yard. It charged me, *hommie.* It broke through my fence, *ese.* The bull smashed against the door, destroying my porch. It pounded against the door, cracking it. Then it disappeared. All of sudden this naked white devil with horns and wings was flying above me. It tried to grab me, but its hands went through me. Somehow, I wrestled it to the floor. I cried out to Jesus, but I doubted myself. Was I paying for my sins? But I'm not evil, *hommie.* I slashed the devil's throat with my angel blade. Then this little girl came out of the white demon's bleeding neck. She was crying. She had been trying to escape. She reached out to me. I held her, like I'm holding you now because a demon is trying to possess me for stealing her away. Help me, *hommie*. Help me."

Danny's face paled ghost white. He looked courageously terrified. He resembled someone who had been beaten with a logging chain. And then he passed out.

"What the hell's going on?" I asked Soto.

"Danny nodded out."

"How the fuck did he float to the ceiling?" I asked.

"That mother-fucker just got back from Chichén Itzá with his cousin, where they were shooting too much Mexican Mud and chewing mushrooms, and playing around with Palo Mayombe. He's been learning some universal language called Esperanto," Soto explained. "How the fuck should I know. Crazy *vato's* been levitating since we were kids."

"Who's the teenager?"

"I don't know," Tony answered pissed-off. The teenage girl didn't say a word or stir as she silently slept.

"Danny! Danny! Get your ass up, you juju, junkie mother-fucker! Come on, get up! Get the fuck out of here!" Soto commanded, nudging Danny with his foot. I went to the girl and quietly knelt beside her. As I stared into her face she felt my breath mix with hers and she opened her eyes. She had deep green eyes, with auburn lines running through them, leading to brown pupils. Her hair was bright, brick-red with a slight white streak running through it. Her body and nose were slender and her smile was full and embracing. When she opened her eyes she didn't look like a teenager, but more like a woman: an honest, noble, sexy woman. She reached out and held my chin with one hand and pulled my face to hers. She whispered in my ear, her lips brushing through my hair. "I know you. I know all about you," she proclaimed. And I believed her.

Danny sat up, scrubbed his face, lifted himself off the floor by his hair, apologized, shook Tony's hand, and thanked him. Then he recognized me for the first time. *"Orale, ese.* What's up, *hommie?"* Danny asked with tired eyes, shaking my hand while he continued to scrub his face. "The compulsive urges of the thoughtless grow like a creeper. They jump like a monkey from one life to another, looking for fruit in the forest," Danny said to me, reciting a line from the Dhammapada. "Ok... Ok... Later, *hommies."* Danny stumbled out the door. I turned around to say goodbye to the girl/woman but she was already gone.

"What the fuck happened to you that night? I haven't seen you since...How long?" Soto asked, giving me a bear hug. "You want a vodka or Scotch? That's what you drink, right?"

"Vodka."

"What's it been, fifteen, twenty years?"

"Something like that," I answered.

But we spoke a couple of times on the telephone and bumped into each other at a Black Flag reunion concert, but we hadn't spent any significant time together since we last hung out at the Rose Bowl with a bunch of punk friends twenty years ago.

Soto was a tall, lanky, tatted-up punk back then and we had just graduated from high school. Now he was a tall, buffed out, tatted-up, long-hair slinging dope and rod busting for the Iron Workers Union, Local 416. He'd been in and out of prison for assault narcotics and drunk driving, and he was most likely still a snap case.

Me and about six friends had been drinking at the Rose Bowl after 2:00 a.m. when Joey, the toughest and meanest punk we knew, (nevertheless, our friend), came up behind Tony and innocently tapped him on the shoulder, greeting him, "Hey man, what's up?" Tony turned around and punched Joey in the nose, splitting it wide open. Joey flew back, but he was caught by a retaining wall. Soto, surprised by whom he'd just laid out, went over too Joey, cradling his bleeding face with both hands, holding it in a gentle and nurturing manner, apologizing, "Dude. I'm sorry. I'm so sorry. I didn't know it was you, man." And just as we all stood suspended in Soto's heartfelt sorrow for busting Joey's nose, Soto continued, "Joey, Dude. I'm sorry. I didn't know it was you... But... But... It's too late now." Then Soto proceeded to pound Joey's face, over-and-over-and-over again, until Joey passed out. When Soto snapped out of his logical reaction he turned around and snatched a beer with his bloody hand.

One might ask, "Why was Soto's reaction logical?"

Once Joey's eyes stopped watering from having his nose busted, he would have beat the shit out of Soto. Soto had to act while he had the upper hand, even though he made a mistake. At this point Soto had to show everyone how crazy he was so no one would jump him, siding with Joey. Last man standing and all that shit.

Hanging out with Soto was a coin toss. You never knew if he was going to give you a big hug and hand you a drink, or if he was going punch you in the face. I was glad that he was offering me a vodka, and I didn't want to talk about the last night we hung out. So I told him I moved to the east coast.

I asked him if he knew where I could find Lucy and Angie.

Clinical, Brutal....

"You and Angie use to romp," he reminded me. "She's not the same girl she used to be."

"I'm not the same guy I used to be."

"The fuck you aren't..."

Just as Soto was about to remind me of my troubled past Lucy and Angie walked in. They had just escaped from Prototype Rehab for women, where the speed freaks obsessively cleaned the place and drank strong coffee, while the heroin addicts lounged around reading books and discussed politics and drug statistics.

Morris and Anina were with Lucy and Angie. In the past Morris kept Lucy warm as they slept in an alley near Temple and Alvarado, in East Hollywood, while Anina and Angie prostituted themselves to support all four of their addictions. Morris was a large, tall black man, who always behaved and spoke like a gentleman. Lucy attempted prostitution, charging only forty dollars per fuck. She had one taker: a spindly *vato* named Spider from 18th Street. After him she was only offered four-dollars by lowlife junkies desperate to find out if they could still screw. Her career as a whore lasted three days, so she settled for Morris' comforting arms. Anina and Angie were able to pull thirty dollars for head and sixty-plus dollars per fuck.

Morris and Anina were hoping to cop some Mexican Mud from Soto who wasn't interested in Talley Sticks or Fractional Reserve Lending. All he gave them was a dime-bag of Mexican Rose and a large can of Mannitol, which they could trade for some pills with a dealer in Down Town L.A. Then they were on their way.

(Mannitol is a milk sugar used as a baby laxative and is commonly used to cut heroin with.)

I had sat patiently feeling the hole in my stomach expanding, which was molested by a natural frustration in the soul. Lucy and Angie thanked Anina and Morris for giving them a ride from Pomona. Then Angie recognized me. We stared motionlessly at each other, missing all the years between us. I thought of Abraham Heschel writing in *Man Is Not Alone*, "It is incumbent on us to obtain the perception of life eternal in everyday deeds." The time Angie and I spent apart suspended our shared experiences, which were never temporal. They were like cracks in the floor of heaven, illuminating images of what could be. We were each other's center and the world revolved around our tender yet desperate dreams for one another. These two girls were everlasting in me, and Angie would always be the girl who reminded me of the infinite possibilities.

Lucy and Soto stood quietly watching Angie and me silently reacquainting ourselves. Then Soto had enough, "He's still the same jack-off he was when we were kids."

Lucy hugged me as if she were holding herself together with my arms. The roles had reversed, because Lucy and Angie had kept me from going out of my mind when we were young. Many times they yanked me back over the railing of the Eaton Canyon Bridge, or slapped my father's snub-nose .357 – with one bullet in it – out of my hand, or picked me up from a puddle of puke and blood and tossed me in a cold bath. I wasn't trying to kill myself, I was just a drunken-drugged-out-adrenaline junkie, at least that's what I told myself.

Lucy and Angie got me out of the neighborhood and talked to me about art, books, travel and philosophy. When we were in high school the three of us use to take off to Arizona or northern California. The two of them use to read to me. I'd ask them the meaning of words and concepts. I had never read an entire book until I was seventeen: Hemingway's *Farewell To Arms*. It was the first and one of the few books to invoke a physical emotion in me. Lucy and Angie talked about how a book could scare them or make them cry or laugh or reflect on themselves or discover a world they knew nothing about. I was too busy getting high and hadn't the faintest idea that the written word could incite such personal meaning. These two girls mothered me into a new life and now they were tore up. Their bodies were ravaged from all the dope they injected.

Lucy had abscesses all over her body from shooting speed and heroin. She was inflicted with Bells Palsy while kicking heroin in the Glendale Jail, but she hadn't noticed it until she was released. She went to a Thrifty Drug Store and bought an ice cream. The first lick slid out of her mouth. She caught a bus, wondering what was going wrong with her face. The bus driver watched her, in his rearview mirror, having a difficult time with the ice-cream dripping out of the left side of her mouth and on her shirt. Two Armenian girls were laughing. So Lucy looked at herself in the reflection of the bus window. She couldn't believe she had lost her smile.

Angie had contracted HIV from hooking or slamming dope. She was never quite sure from which, but she suspected that she rigged it by sharing a needle with a crippled male prostitute, who died two years later from AIDS. But she still looked gorgeous.

Angie and I use to make love in the back seat of the Lucy's car as she drove us around. I always had a bag of coke or some weed, Angie always had money, and Lucy had a car. All three of us had an appetite for anything that wasn't in the neighborhood, trying to escape the sweat of our streets. We were inseparable for three years and then I left.

I went through a fanatical religious phaze. It was my way of getting clean. Lucy was accepted to UCLA, where she majored in psychology and got strung out on speed, believing she was born into the Illuminati only she hadn't actualized her privileges yet. She thought the Illuminati would contact her when she had attained some secret knowledge, so she followed every white car on the freeway with a half ounce of meth tucked in her bra. She did this until Aleida, her Mexican psychic gave her the whammy and set her straight. Angie decided to follow Marco Polo's Silk Route, only she never made it past West Hollywood, where she got strung out. All three of us went through a two year period where we lived in a cheating confusion which we never resolved but found our way out of. Then Lucy and Angie found each other again, whereas, I moved to Boston and then to New York and then to Spain and Italy and then to Oklahoma and Northern California. Now I was back in L.A.

The first time Lucy stuck a needle in her arm was at a Latvian dance convention in Long Beach. Angie slammed her first dose in the bathroom at the Whisky-A-Go-Go, during a Faster Pussycat show. I never put a needle in my arm, and Soto only sold the stuff in between Union jobs. The four of us had a few drinks. Angie and I didn't say a word to each other. We just caught each other in between missing glimpses that said everything that was necessary for the time.

Lucy's car was in Soto's garage so I asked her and Angie for a ride.

As we drove to Pasadena I told them about Tino. Lucy was always the most inquisitive and wanted to know as much as she could about Tino. Angie was looking extremely tired. She held my hand as she tried to stay awake.

Tino had been a rich kid who was educated at Eton and went to Oxford to study linguistics and began studying copies of Sumerian clay cuneiform texts. His parents owned a veranda outside of Barcelona where Tino spent his vacations. When he graduated from Oxford with a Master's in Linguistics he moved to Los Angeles where he landed a job rewriting scripts until he went from chipping to becoming a full blown addict. When his parents died he shot half his inheritance up his arm. One night after the Domino's Pizza boy left, delivering ribs and a six pack of Mountain Dew, he shot a heavy dose and passed out for two days. When he woke up he discovered that he had no feeling in his left arm. He rushed to the emergency, where the doctors explained that he had killed all the nerves in his arm and that it would have to be amputated. He asked if there was another solution. There was, but it was experimental and costly. Tino sunk the rest of his inheritance into saving the arm that he used to mainline in. The doctors sent him to Chicago where bionics were implanted in his arm. Then they waited, hoping he would not contract any infections, which he did and was forced to amputate the arm anyway. The loss of his arm was a daily reminder that he had become a junkie who would never get as high as he did the first time.

When he returned to L.A. he started using the other arm to shoot coke in the morning and heroin throughout the day, until he nodded out too many times, so he'd shoot more coke and then slam a large dose of heroin to sleep. He did this for three years. Then he was arrested and sent to County Jail for six months. During this time his girlfriend od'd and Tino fell into a depression that he never recovered from. He cleaned up for about six years.

A friend of ours, who worked in the movie industry, would use on his down time and got pretty strung-out. Tino tried to help him clean-up, but Tino just started using with him. He's been at it hard, now, for seven years.

Lucy was excited by Tino's story. When we got to Tino's office her panties were wet, and she pulled them off to prove it.

Angie fell asleep in my arms as I read Wu Ch'Êng-Ên's *Monkey* to her. She felt free and independent, with no worries as if she had been carved out of stone and brought to life by a warm, tender wind. She looked peacefully lost, waiting to leave this world; not anxious; just ready. When she woke, she asked me if I would shoot her. I resisted having never done anything like that before. She assured me it was easy and "not as frightening as when we were children getting immunized." She sat close to me and whispered on my lips that she wanted it to be me. I understood perfectly what was about to happen. Lucy and I both knew what was going on. Tino no longer felt that he was alone. All four us knew. But I was having a difficult time accepting it.

I walked outside and lit a cigarette. Lucy followed me and explained that Angie was ridiculously tired of being sick, and that both of them believed it wasn't a coincidence we had found each other that day, or that Tino had brought us together.

"You don't know what the fuck you're talking about. Three lonely junkies, that's all," I said lying to myself.

"That's right. But you're the loneliest person I have ever known. I know you're up for this." Lucy reached for my cigarette then took a drag.

Clinical, Brutal....

"This is why I woke up this morning? This is the Reason I got out of bed today, to do this?"

"That's right, Reason with a capital R, you got it. I been taking care of her all these years and now you're here to do this," Lucy explained with a gentle, appreciating tone.

We smoked the rest of my cigarette together in silence. Then we went inside, where Angie and Tino were preparing their syringes with large doses of black tar heroin. Tino mixed his with cocaine.

I couldn't take my eyes off of Angie. Her slender frame, long legs, small breasts, beautiful brown hair, penetrating green eyes, elfish ears and smile reminded me of the time when I first felt the autumn winds. She took hold of my sleeve, tugging me towards her. Lucy leaned over and hugged her with tears in her eyes, whispering her ever constant love for Angie. Then Lucy pulled away and followed Tino into the bathroom.

Angie and I sank into the center of the sofa. She kissed me between my eyes and slid her lips down to mine. We pulled ourselves deeper into each other. Our lips felt like the first time we kissed, when we were naïve, believing we would become who we'd always dreamt of, but we'd never developed the discipline to manifest those dreams. Nevertheless, it was a peaceful moment with no longings or surprises.

Angie positioned her arm on my lap and tightened a lavender tie around it. She showed me where to stick the needle. When her vein surfaced I stuck it sensitively. I pulled back on the plunger a little, watching her blood flow into the syringe. We sat in suspension, exchanging our lost years for one more innocent moment shared together. The ethereal hovered over us. We found ourselves in another kiss as I slowly released the brown mud that would never give me back the girl I once knew. I felt her final touch for one last time as she rushed through me. Then she disappeared.

I sat with her head in my lap for about fifteen minutes. I felt empty and quiet. There were no invasive thoughts... Nothing... Just a still and silent presence.

I heard Lucy washing up in the bathroom. I set Angie's head gently on the sofa and got up to snap a shot of Tino in his everlasting slumber with Lucy's wet panties tied around his one remaining arm.

Then I sat back down next to Angie returning her head to my lap. Lucy sat next to me combing her fingers through Angie's hair. We didn't say a word for about an hour. Then she knelt beside Angie in a solemn fashion and whispered on Angie's parted lips, "Angie, you're my favorite."

Lucy and I looked at each other as if asking, "What do we do now?" But the answer revealed itself before we had the chance to ask. We exchanged our lifeless dueling kisses for Angie's animating kiss. Then we left like a couple of feral alley cats, dragging courage behind us tied to our broken tails.

An alternative version of 'Rubber-Hose Real Estate' first appeared in 'Exquisite Corpse.'

Clinical, Brutal....

Teleny

Radcliff Gregory

Teleny, Bibliophile (part I)

It began in a fervent circle,
with a flurry of fingers
that dived down between words,
eking fiction from friction.

Their words circled and hovered,
until, finally, all eyes glistened on me;
one shaking hand caressed my spine,
slithering down, down, beneath cloth,

slipping expert fingers where none had been before,
inching inwards and upwards,
forcing me wide open,
waiting for the first, inevitable splatter

     of ink against paper.
One by one, men cracked me wide,
grunting glyphs into calfskin,
igniting the coal to spit back their spend.

- - - - - - - - -- - - - -- - - - - - - - -- - - - - - - - - -- - - - - - - -- - - - -

Teleny, Bibliophile (part II)

Each *lingua Franca* lingers,
groin brushing my head,
softly aware of sheathed vellum,
but not its hand-swap of secrets.

Some men thrust out a card,
take me in hand, down their trousers;
they walk gingerly through London's
most talked-about streets.

Sometimes, I would be the evening's devotion
of one man, squinting behind closed drapes,
unclothing me with relish,
skipping pages, fevered eyes scanning.

Sometimes I would be the party trick;
one tongue probing for select words
while others tipped the brandy.
Curiosity made them brutish;

they would stare and grab at me,
forcing me wider open to take them all,
one after the other, till my spine cracked,
my face jaded and sagging,
too weary to resist or keep it shut.
They sucked each word off the page,

Clinical, Brutal....

gulped it down, before spitting it
into another waiting mouth,

until they bored of my musty taste.
Then they would clothe me again,
return me in shuffling silence,
already forming their intimacies
into jolly tales for born-again buggerados.

PAPANICOLAOU TEST:
A GRAND GUIGNOL

By Díre McCain

CHARACTERS:

Uxor

Dr. Art(thur) Sterben, Ob/Gyn

Rudolf Ludwig Karl Virchow

SETTING:

Newport Beach, California, United States of America

****

Biological Clock
Noun
1) **The progression or time period from puberty to menopause, marking a woman's ability to bear children.**

2) **The defective gene that drives a woman to blindly obsess over procreating by a certain age, regardless of whether or not she's fit to be a mother.**

****

"Gimme that People magazine, Arthur."

*Every time you call me Arthur I want to belt you across the face and fracture your mandible, so you will desist once and for all. It is **Art**, not Arthur. It has always been Art, but the instant I acquiesced to your incessant hounding and placed that three-carat diamond on your digitus* *medicinalis, it became Arthur. It drives me out of my fucking mind, but you refuse to stop, no matter how many times I have begged...*

"The one with Oprah on the cover. Here, gimme it."

Ah yes, your guru, even though you are a flagrant racist, who comes from a long line of flagrant racists. How would you function in this world without her? God forbid if you had to form your own opinions, and make decisions for yourself. If that egomaniacal brainwasher commanded you to spread feces all over your face, like cold cream, and go out in public, you would do it, you obtuse cunt...

Art(hur) picks up the magazine and tosses it to his wife.

"Woah! Doesn't Angelina Jolie look super hot? I can't believe she just had twins!"

*The inspiration behind that banal, gaudy coccyx tattoo that you so proudly draw attention to at every given opportunity. Also responsible for your ostensible and hypocritical fascination with sapphism. We both know that you are the biggest homophobe who has ever walked the face of the earth, but now that it is **voguish** to be a **pseudo**-lesbian, you **love** dykes, except for my sister, of course, who is a **real** lesbian...*

"And don't forget we have to be at the Jones' in an hour."

How could I possibly forget, you insufferable nag? You have only been reminding me once every five minutes since I crawled across the threshold into this intolerable self-imposed prison from my exhausting job, which steals hours of my life, all so you can squander the lion's share of my arduously earned dollars at Fascist Island and that extortionate day spa. If you only knew how badly I would like to chop off that garishly streaked hair, and yank out those hideous French pedicured ungues at the eponychium with a pair of tenaculum forceps. And do not get me started on the wardrobe. There is a plethora of usuriously expensive designer clothing in that closet that you have not worn so much as once, yet you continue to acquire more and more on a weekly basis...

"Better start getting ready now, Arthur. Just TiVo that stupid fight, and watch it later. I'll never understand why you like all that violence anyway."

That is too rich, coming from a woman who has a long history of domestic violence against men. When the queen hydra doesn't get her way, the retractable fangs appear, ravenous for vital fluids. I should have heeded Richard's warnings, the lucky bastard. He must be counting his blessings every day since you pulled your venomous fangs out of him and dug them into my carotid artery. But of course, you are an abject coward when dealing with your own gender, because they may strike back, which would be terrifically just. A fractured nasal bridge and zygomatic bone would be the most effective treatment for your disease, you sadistic bitch. If only I could write a prescription...

"David's super excited to show you the work he had done on the back bathroom. He's totally hip on the latest trends in interior design. You need to take a lesson from him."

Art(hur) glances up at his wife, who's fervently flipping through the deceitful pabulumzine, eagerly swallowing every word and image, as though it's gospel. He lets out a cough of disgust, then picks up his coffee mug, takes a few swigs, and places it back down on the coaster.

David is a pompous, mind-numbingly boring dick. Hate the son of a bitch. I have not one thing in common with him, but since his uptight cunt of a wife is your best friend, I am forced to act as though I like the patrician bastard, and that I give a shit about his god damn renovations. Him and his daddy's money. Of course he's hip on the latest trends,

Clinical, Brutal....

because he has no idea how it is to be forced to work for a living, and neither do you. God, I knew that marrying you was a monumental mistake, serves me right for seeing dollar signs. I should have known that your father was a fucking miser when he refused to pick up the check the night I met him. Oh god, what I would give to be able to go back, and know what I know now ...

"Okay, Arthur, are you listening to me?"

*I cannot help but listen to you, because your voice is like a god damn magpie, cawing incessantly. Try as I may, I cannot tune you out. Even when you are on the other side of the country, I can still **feel** that agonizingly shrill voice, reverberating in my primary auditory cortex. Caw, caw, caw, caw, caw, caw, caw, caw, caw, caw, caw ...*

"Because I have something super important to tell you. I was gonna to wait till tomorrow, but the excitement is killing me!"

Oh no, here we go again. I wonder how much it's going to set me back this time, you useless parasite ...

"It's super exciting! Here, put this back."

Art(hur) takes the magazine from his wife's hand and tosses is back on to the coffee table.

I am certain it's just thrilling, I am on the edge of my seat, and of course, it cannot wait until this round is over. You must tell me right this instant, mustn't you...

"Are you ready?"

I will never be ready, or responsive, but you will tell me regardless ...

"I'm pregnant!"

Marriages are not normally made to avoid having children.

Art(hur) looks up at his wife, visibly stunned.

*Jesus fucking Christ! No! No! No! Those words did **not** just pour out of your rima oris!*

"Didn't you hear me, Arthur? I said, I'm pregnant! Isn't that like the most super thing you've ever heard?"

Art(hur) continues to stare at his wife, now blankly, as though in a daze.

If the man of science chose to follow the example of historians and pulpit-orators, and to obscure strange and peculiar phenomena by employing a hollow pomp of big and sounding words, this would be his opportunity, for we have approached one of the greatest mysteries which surround the problem of animated nature and distinguish it above all other problems of science. To discover the relations of man and woman to the egg-cell would be almost equivalent of the egg-cell in the body of the mother, the transfer to it by means of the seed, of the physical and mental characteristics of the father, affect all the questions which the human mind has ever raised in regard to existence.

*You scheming cunt! This was all planned! Oh god, why did I agree to fuck you that night? You repulse me, you adulterous whore! It was a god damn miracle I was able to achieve an erection in the first place, never mind maintain it, while sloshing about in that maculate, cavernous vagina of yours! I should have known that you were lying about taking the Tri-Cyclen! You were probably taking Clomid instead! And I bet it was my bitch partner who gave it to you! God damn it! I made it perfectly clear at the outset of this unbearable misalliance that I did **not** want any children! Have you no mercy at all? How on earth* *can you even consider dragging an innocent child into this multi-car train wreck with **you** in the conductor's seat?*

"Aren't you gonna say anything, Arthur?"

Art(hur) remains silent, his gaze now affixed to the cartoonishly airbrushed portrait of his wife that's hanging over the wall unit.

"I hate you! You're totally impossible! I'm having this baby, with or without your blessings! Besides, you have no say! It's *my* body!"

> **Only those who regard healing as the ultimate goal of their efforts can, therefore, be designated as physicians.**

Without uttering a single word, Art(hur) goes into the bedroom and retrieves a loaded Smith & Wesson Model 500 from the nightstand. He then returns to the living room, grabs his wife by the throat, slams her to the ground, and pulls up her dress, completely ignoring her bewildered screams. After ripping off her obscenely overpriced size five Cosabella lace panties – that were already bursting at the seams, struggling to accommodate her size seven ass – he methodically spreads apart her labia, and shoves the barrel up into her cervical canal, like a speculum, then pulls the trigger four times.

Looming over her twitching body, he instantly falls into a state of suspended animation, pondering whether he should fellate the 8-3/8" barrel and suck out that last spermatozoon, or shoot it up into the primigravida's lead-filled womb.

Eleven minutes and twenty-three seconds later, he snaps out of it.

Leaving the gun embedded in her warm, yet lifeless and prolapsed uterus, he goes into the kitchen, removes a pint of Häagen-Dazs Butter Pecan from the freezer, and a tablespoon from the silverware drawer, then returns to the living room to watch the last three rounds of the fight before retiring for the night.

Disease is not something personal and special, but only a manifestation of life under modified conditions, operating according to the same laws as apply to the living body at all times, from the first moment until death.

****

omnis cellula e cellula

Clinical, Brutal....

FRENZY OF THE FLESH

Stewart Home

Steve Queen suffered from an aversion to freedom. It was a deep seated need to pursue his artistic inclinations that had forced him to leave the sleepy village of Burnham in Buckinghamshire. The teenager had enjoyed his strict Methodist upbringing and now that he found himself in a student hostel, he felt lost and alone.

Steve lived for the precious hours he spent in his studio. As long as he was moving a pencil over paper, the youth felt contented. Sometimes after completing a life study, Steve would look at his work and feel repulsed. From childhood, the belief that there was no pleasure to be taken in the nude female form had been instilled in the teenager's mind. Occasionally, the tutors provided a male model. When that happened Queen felt an unfamiliar stirring in his groin.

The art school Steve was attending, the De Sade, was one of the most prestigious in Britain. Located on London's Gower Street, it was situated between Bloomsbury and Fitzrovia, two of the plusher areas of the capital's West End. On his arrival, Queen had been distressed to discover that many of his fellow students were bohemians. Most found it next to impossible to get up before midday. They'd spend the afternoon nursing coffees in the college cafeteria, while evenings were frittered away drinking in trendy clubs like the Limelight and the Wag. Nights were a time for bonking rather than sleep. Any lulls in this schedule were roughly divided between reading Viz, watching tv and doing the odd sketch.

Steve, who got up at five-thirty in the morning to say his

prayers, was considered the epitome of squaresville by his fellow students. The Tuesday of the Queen's third week at the De Sade seemed no different to any of the other days he'd spent at the college. Steve had taken a break at ten. He'd gone to the cafeteria to get a glass of milk and a buttered roll. As the teenager tucked into his modest fare, John Thomas – a world famous performance artist who taught in the mixed media department – came and sat beside him.

'Fresher?' Thomas enquired.

'Yes,' Steve replied.

'What department are you in?' Thomas demanded.

'Painting,' Steve replied.

'You need to be filled with poison,' Thomas announced. 'When I've finished my coffee, we'll head over to my studio and start work on it. I've got this feeling about you, I sincerely believe that you could be the greatest artist since Van Gogh! But if you're to be anything, you've got to be filled with poison.'

'You're the teacher, you know best,' Steve's father had beaten respect for authority into his son.

John Thomas had a tried and tested formula for seducing freshers. The first thing he did was make Queen swallow a tab of White Lightning. The acid would take half an hour to hit. In the meantime, Thomas decided to prepare Steve for the performance ritual. This would, of course, be fully documented.

'Take your clothes off,' Thomas instructed.

'I can't,' Queen replied.

'Why not?' Thomas demanded.

'I'm embarrassed,' Steve mumbled.

'Look,' Thomas hissed, 'if you wanna be a great artist, you'll have to bare your soul to the public. If you're too uptight to take your clothes off in front of me, then you'll never cut it as a genius.'

Thomas had a way with words. Before he'd even finished speaking, Queen had begun to undress.

'What's that for?' Steve enquired pointing at a bath full of rotting meat.

'That's for our performance,' Thomas explained. 'But don't worry about that yet. I'll have to get you prepared first.'

When Queen had removed all his clothing, Thomas took a large jar of Vaseline and began to rub the petroleum jelly onto the fresher's face, hands, genitals, feet and then finally into his arse. Steve had a hard-on throughout the operation. After this, Thomas took a roll of gauze and bandaged the youth's face, hands and feet. As his teacher started work on the genitals, Steve's erection was really throbbing. The gauze was wrapped around Steve's balls. Then with expert precision, Thomas wound the bandage around the teenager's straining love muscle. Steve could stand it no longer. He shot off a wad of his genetic dew. The liquid DNA hit the art teacher in the eye, dripped down the side of his face and into his mouth. Thomas was a professional and continued his bandaging as if nothing had happened.

At last the preparations were finished, the gauze secured with a safety pin. Thomas removed his own clothing and used the internal telephone system to summon a technical assistant. The technician was wearing a white coat. Steve couldn't see this because a bandage had been wrapped over his eyes. There was a gap in the gauze to allow for the use of his mouth, but otherwise his head and neck were completely covered by the bandage.

The White Lightning was beginning to hit as Thomas

manoeuvred Steve into the tub filled with rotting meat. The youth's mind was filled with a pure white light. It was as if he'd entered heaven. He felt weightless and filled with well-being. Thomas positioned Steve face up in the bath and then got in on top of him. He sat so that his shit chute was positioned over Steve's mouth.

Queen began to lick the arsehole. He didn't connect the taste in his mouth with the sweet smell of the sewers. His acid-armed consciousness had convinced him that he was in heaven. Thomas took a Tibetan ceremonial knife and cut into Steve's flesh. The fresher experienced his skin being ripped apart as a sweet caress. As Queen's tongue lashed into Thomas's arse, the wayward art teacher began to masturbate. Thomas shot off a wad of liquid genetics and then rubbed the DNA into the wounds he'd sliced out of the youth's body.

The art teacher twisted around and shoved his love muscle into Steve's mouth, then picked up a lump of rotting meat and rubbed it all over his body. The fresher sucked his teacher's throbbing member deep into his throat. Queen had retreated to a point beyond consciousness. Although he'd been sexually repressed for every second of his waking life, now that his erotic energies were released, he knew instinctively how to deal with the uncut meat that had been stuffed into his mouth.

Thomas was out on the mudflats. He experienced the smell of rotting meat, wafting up from beneath him, as a salty breeze blown across from a tropical sea. Steve pumped up the volume and Thomas experienced orgasm as a DNA encoded replay of the first star exploding. The art teacher flipped Queen around, the fresher's arsehole was well greased and Thomas had no trouble penetrating the sphincter. The top then shoved a piece of rotting meat into Queen's mouth before biting into the student's shoulder. The technician was getting perfect shots on his camcorder.

Thomas was an old hand at the bump and grind routine. But young boys tended to get him over-excited. The art teacher was the wrong side of forty and to be making it with someone still at the peak of physical perfection really turned him on. Thomas came far quicker than he'd planned. An ego-negating simultaneous orgasm drained the last ounce of energy from the performance art perverts. They had reached that peak from which man and man can never jointly return.

Dave Smith was a youth of simple tastes. He didn't ask for much in life. Just a boyfriend who liked getting it eight times a night, a wad of cash in his pocket and the opportunity to spend, spend, SPEND!

Dave thought art was a load of bullshit. A bourgeois mental set leading to an irrational reverence for activities that suited ruling class needs. Still, his art master at school had considered him a brilliant colourist. A college career had seemed less hassle to Dave than getting a job. Bunking off on a fine art degree course without loss of income was less problematic than skiving on some underpaid government training scheme. And the money was better too! It was a logical following through of these considerations that brought Dave to the De Sade.

Dave liked London, it was a damn sight better than the sleepy village he'd left behind in the Cotswolds. What Smith didn't dig was having to share a room with a religious fanatic who objected to his all night fuck sessions. Steve Queen was a killjoy. He didn't like partying, hanging out on Old Compton Street or sex. The only things he was into were religion and art – and in Dave's mind there wasn't much difference between them.

Justin Pitt-Simmons was a sadist with a difference. When it

came to love relationships, such as the one he was having with Dave Smith, he liked to be beaten up rather than doing the beating. He would only vent his sadistic streak on total strangers – and quite often this meant going to murder and beyond. Justin was a militant anti-smoker. His victims were always nicotine addicts who he tortured to death with their own cigarettes.

Justin had been seeing Dave for a week. To date they'd always made love in Justin's shared student room or out in the street. Pitt-Simmons got off on total strangers walking in on his love making, but with his room-mate it had become so common-place that it was no longer stimulating. And so Justin had insisted that he be taken back to his boyfriend's room. Pitt-Simmons got his way, and although he'd not met Dave's room-mate, he knew the bastard was a religious fanatic. It made him horny just to think about that Jesus freak walking in on them.

Dave was beating out the primitive rhythm of sex. He loved the 'scent' of Justin's arsehole. His partner experienced ecstasy as Dave's huge cock penetrated his sphincter. They were no longer in London. The sexual stimulation had activated genetic codings buried deep inside their brains. Their movements were under the Dictatorship of the DNA. Dave and Justin were basking on the mudflats of prehistory.

Steve Queen and John Thomas were midway into another art action. They'd been experimenting with ritual performances for more than a month. The white coated video technician had recorded all their work for detailed study by posterity. Queen was strung by his feet from the ceiling, his hands were chained to the floor and blood was rushing to his head. In front of him was a video screen. From upside down, he was watching a play-back of an earlier action he'd made with John.

Clinical, Brutal....

Thomas was beating out the primitive rhythm of sex. He was holding onto Steve's ankles, his arms stretched out above his head. The art teacher was looking beyond the video screen, into a mirror he'd placed behind it. He studied his reflection as he moved in and out of Steve's arsehole.

Thomas wanted to destroy Steve's sense of identity. The action had reached a crucial stage. During their previous rituals, the youth had been drugged and blindfolded. This was the first time Steve had seen any of his performances played back on video. He was about to discover it wasn't always Thomas who'd fucked him. On a number of occasions, businessmen had paid for the privilege of screwing the teenager.

Thomas beat harder and brought himself to orgasm, simultaneously shooting a wad of liquid genetics into Steve's tight little arsehole. However, the youth didn't register the orgasm. He was mesmerised by the image of a businessman abusing his body – an episode that was being played back on the video screen.

'You're a rent boy,' Thomas informed him. 'But don't worry, you'll be getting your cut of the loot.'

Steve was overcome by a heady mixture of emotions. He screamed. But the youth also had a hard-on and could feel a strange sexual current surging through his body. He'd been used and abused, cheated and lied to. And yet, seeing that anonymous prick penetrate his sphincter, was a right fucking turn on.

Steve could feel Thomas's hand on his love muscle, beating the meat. He was barely conscious of the liquid genetics that shot from his prick. Cold thoughts had flooded his brain. Thomas wasn't an artist. It was just a cover for his perverted lusts. Steve felt his innocence had been abused. He knew instinctively that once he was unshackled, he'd take his revenge.

'Don't you feel angry?' Thomas enquired trying to fathom the teenager's mood.

'Not at all,' Steve replied, as a controlled rage enabled him to conceal his very real emotions. 'I can see I'm a masochist. I can only thank you for what you've done. You've helped me discover my innermost feelings!'

'In that case,' Thomas replied, 'I'll unshackle you and we'll go out for a meal to celebrate. I've always wanted my very own sex slave!'

Once Steve was unchained, he leapt at Thomas and pushed him against the end wall of the studio. The white coated video technician filmed every second of the action as Steve beat his teacher's head against the brick wall until there was nothing left of it but a study in blood, pulp and gore.

Once Thomas was dead and his limp body had sunk to the floor, Steve felt a calmness descend upon him. He turned around and looked at the video technician, who was still filming him.

'What are you gonna do with the footage you've shot?' Steve demanded.

'I'll deposit it with my lawyer for safe keeping,' the technician replied. 'You're a very great artist but this film can't be shown while you're alive. If it was, you'd end up in jail.'

'Will you help me avoid punishment for my crime?' Steve asked.

'Once I've stored this and all the other videos safely, I'll come back here and dispose of the body,' the video technician announced as he removed a VHS cassette from his camcorder.

'Do you really think I'm a great performance artist?' Steve

enquired.

'Of course,' the technician replied. 'Your teacher was a fake but you're for real.'

Steve walked over to the technician and the two men embraced. They kissed passionately and rubbed their crotches together.

'We can't make performance art here,' the video technician whispered. 'It doesn't seem right.'

'We'll meet up in my room,' Steve shot back. 'If you can just sort out the mess here first.'

'No problem.' the youth's new performance art partner assured him.

'Got any fags?' Steve wanted to know.

'I didn't know you smoked,' the technician replied hauling three packets of Camel cigarettes from his bag and then handing them to Queen.

The teenager took the smokes and kissed the technician.

'Every genius needs an addictive habit,' Steve explained. 'Smoking is the least unchristian one I can think of, so I'm taking it up.'

The two men embraced again and then parted.

Dave and Justin were doing a 69 when they heard Steve's key in the lock. Justin was really thrilling to the primitive rhythm of sex and as Steve walked into the room, he shot off a wad of liquid genetics. The spunk that Dave managed to avoid swallowing was spilling out the side of his mouth. But everything was ruined when Justin realised that Queen was puffing on a cigarette. Justin could feel his asthma coming on and simultaneously, a sense of all the injustices he'd suffered welled up inside him. What right did this creep have to spoil his fun? He'd looked forward to the Jesus freak walking in on him as he made love to his boyfriend. But in his wildest dreams, Justin had never imagined the bastard would be a smoker!

Steve lay down on his bed, flicked ash onto the floor. He'd said nothing to Dave and Justin, not even hello. He was lost in his own private thoughts, thinking of the technician whose name he didn't even know – and the art action the two of them were going to make together.

Dave was well aware that Justin had been turned off by the smell of nicotine. He simply wanted to carry on with the sexual athletics but knew this was out of the question until Justin had taken his revenge. He rolled free of Justin, enabling his partner to get up from the bed.

Steve made no effort to resist when Justin hauled him up from his pit. He knew Dave's boyfriend was an art student, so he figured it was alright for the two of them to make some kind of performance action together. Steve didn't even protest when Justin strapped his hands to the light fitting and his legs to the beds that flanked two sides of the room.

Justin ripped Steve's clothes from him. Beneath the thin veil of Steve's Christian morality there was a pagan lust for nude encounters of every kind. A lust that was revealed in Steve's smile and throbbing erection. Justin searched the pockets of the clothes he'd torn from his victim's body and found three packets of Camels – two sealed and one opened. A box of matches completed his haul.

Justin lit a cigarette and stubbed it out on the rim of Steve's arse. His victim squealed in delight. Queen was enjoying this art action. It reminded him of the sessions he'd had with John Thomas.

Justin relit the cigarette, crawled under his victim, then pulled the bastard's mouth open and stubbed the gasper out on Steve's tongue.

Justin lit fag after fag, extinguishing them in Queen's ears, mouth and up his nose. As Justin proceeded with the torture session, Steve let out little cries of pleasure. He had not yet caught onto the fact that this was not an art action, that this was for real!

'Your mouth smells like an ashtray!' Justin spat. 'You're just a nicotine addled shitbag, who'd die of lung cancer in a few years if I hadn't decided to put you out of your misery. Your life is nothing compared to the millions of hours your addiction has taken off other people's lives. Passive smokers suffer illness and death through your selfishness. Aren't you ashamed of all the misery you've caused from smoking on trains, buses, in the streets, pubs, shops and lifts? From smoking at other people's homes and smoking when people come to visit you? From smoking at parties and in toilets? Smoking in bed and in motor cars? Worst of all from smoking in cafes, restaurants and at meal times in general! Destroying your own taste-buds and everyone else's enjoyment of their food!'

Justin paused, then continued with: 'You've not even started suffering yet. I'm gonna teach you the meaning of pain!'

Steve couldn't stifle the beginnings of a giggle.

'What do you think's so funny?' Justin demanded as he stubbed a lighted cigarette on Steve's prick.

'You're going a bit over the top for an art action aren't you? One that's not even being filmed!'

'Do you think I'm joking?' Justin demanded.

'No,' Steve replied. 'Art is a serious business. We're making an art action, it's serious but I think you're hamming it up a bit too much!'

'This isn't a fuckin' art action!' Justin snarled. 'I'm gonna kill you!'

Dave put a copy of Iggy and the Stooges Raw Power onto his hi-fi and turned the volume right up. It would drown out any noise the neighbours might find distracting.

Justin lit four smokes, arranged them in his fist and then stubbed the lot into Queen's groin. This time Steve's scream was for real. The pain was much greater now that he knew Justin wasn't indulging him with a display of performance art bravado. This was for real and reality hurt!

Justin took a lit cigarette and taped the filter to Queen's prick. Steve writhed in agony as the ash burned into his love muscle. He howled but the cries of pain were inaudible over the Stooges body-odour boogie.

Steve could shake ash off his prick but the fag kept burning down towards the filter, leaving an ever lengthening scar on the sensitive flesh of his genetic pump, while his frantic pleas for mercy did nothing to lessen the agony.

Justin opened his bag and took out a packet of fireworks. He inserted several bangers up Queen's arse, leaving one sticking out, ready to be lit. He put bangers into Steve's ears, up Steve's nose, and a fistful into his victim's mouth.

Queen went stiff with fear. Justin moved with the speed of a striking snake, as the flame from his lighter made contact with firework fuse after firework fuse. From the bangers stuck in Steve's nose to the ones jammed into his mouth, then those in the ears – and finally the one that protruded from Queen's arse.

Justin stepped behind the curtains, Dave had already moved back against the door. As the bangers exploded in Steve's nose and mouth, a sheet of flame shot across the room. Then the fireworks in

Queen's ears went off, sending a wave of agony through his brain as his ear drums were blown apart. Steve was dead by the time the shock waves from a final explosion ran up from his arsehole and into his guts, reducing his lower intestines to a bloody pulp.

Justin moved from behind the curtains across to the bed. Dave got on top of the crazed sadist and buggered him to the scorching sound of James Williamson's guitar attack on the Stooges Death Trip.

The technician was banging on the door. He got no response although loud music was blasting from the room. The technician tried the handle and the door opened. When he saw Steve's dead and badly mutilated bulk hanging from the light fitting, deep seated emotions took control of his body. There was an iron lying on the floor. The technician picked it up and smashed it into Dave's skull, killing the art student instantly.

When Dave stopped humping and his body slipped limply from Justin's back, the sadist realised that something was seriously amiss. But the DNA had taken control of his body and his responses were slow. The iron smashed into Justin's head. He was killed by the first blow but the technician kept smashing the blunt instrument into the art student's skull. As he pulped the teenager's brains, the video technician muttered inaudibly that he'd lost his only chance of true love.

The technician could not account for his actions of the previous night. He remembered everything up to seeing Steve's dead body. He knew he'd killed the two guys he'd caught fucking in Steve's room. The blokes he'd done in must have murdered his teenage piece. After that the technician walked aimlessly for hours. Then he'd got hold of some booze. He'd a hell of a hang-over when he woke up.

Worries about the hospital appointment had nagged at the back of the technician's brain for weeks. If it hadn't been for his alcohol induced stupor, he'd have arrived early for the consultation, not late. He'd wanted the results, if only to know the worst. That's what he'd said to the doctor, tell me the worst. And he'd got a straight reply:

'I won't lie to you,' the doctor said, 'the cancer has spread from your lungs and into your bones. There's nothing we can do. Personally, I'd give you a month to live at the most.'

'What did I do to deserve this?' the technician wailed.

'By your own admission, you've smoked forty cigarettes a day for the past fifteen years,' the doctor replied sternly. 'You have only yourself to blame for your condition.'

Previously published in *The Art Strike Handbook* (1989) and *No Pity* (AK Press, 1993).

Clinical, Brutal....

Abandoned Warehouse

A.D.Hitchin

bulbous begging

catches

ripped box

spilling arms,

legs,

hands

feet

with

painted toes

'what the fuck are we doing?'

replacement body parts; syringes and

contraceptives

oven charred black

cock tightly squeezed thrusting deep grimy

mattress

Styrofoam bubbles tattered sense of clarity ash sirens squeal screwing

dirty …

bottle shatters

Written by A.D.Hitchin, 2009

Soho

A.D.Hitchin

Soho. Flashing lights. Cars pass. I smoke. Ember burns neon. Eye egg
whites in doorway ask me if I'm looking for any. What? Cunt. Pussy.
But her make-up is too thick and doesn't fill her crevasses. And she is
too thin; boy-like. Probably heroin or malnutrition. I'd rather fuck a fat
bitch. A fat bitch with a deep juicy cunt. A plump mons pubis.
Something you can bury your face in. Need to escape here. Buildings
closing
in.
Signs flickering. Sex. Cinema. Sex cinema? Bar? Bar under
street, Yes - go underground. Away. Sit in corner. Drink gin. There are
two men in the other corner kissing. Glowing blue under light. Curious I
observe them. Their moist saliva glistening, tongues probing. The way
they grip the hair at the nape of their necks. They probably fuck every
night. No lengthy foreplay or compliments. Just two cocks throbbing,
bursting. Why I always admire prostitutes. There is honesty in them.
The transaction is pure and certain. A 'regular' woman is just a whore
who has not yet admitted it. We are all whores. Wretched slaves and
addicts. Better to confess it. Accept it. God is the hot, moist cunt where
I feel relief. Rare, brief moments of fucking peace. More gin. They are
still tonguing. More gin. I am still watching. More gin? Need to smoke.
Have to leave. Walk
streets.

Written by A.D.Hitchin, 2009.

Clinical, Brutal....

Web-Cam Girl

A.D.Hitchin

I saw something beautiful in her.

Call it clarity, purity or whatever. Yes, she was a web-cam girl. She did work for the 'sex entertainment industry.' But I saw it sparkling through her eyes; lucid and shimmering clear as crystal.

I had just split with my girlfriend when I first met her. I had a vague idea about writing a story concerning internet sex, but truly, I was lonely. The story was just a ruse; a pathetic excuse. The girls were all lined-up in rows on the screen. Green text flashing when they were 'available.' Red when they were 'private.' Blondes, brunettes, red-heads, slim, curvy, fat, white, black, latina, Asian … they were all there under different sections. Their pictures flickering, then disappearing at the roll of a mouse. Somewhere there I saw her. I stopped the page at her long black hair and dark skin. Her eyes brown pools, reaching, clawing …

I logged in and she was laying on a bed looking toward the screen; wearing black lingerie and suspenders. Deep eyes painted with thick kohl lines. The images streamed quickly, her fingernails dancing the keys. The text scrolling below was all foul, some of it almost sub-human. Various anonymous profile predators offering to 'fuck her up the arse', 'cum on her face', 'pound her senseless', 'gangbang her' … you get the picture. One even threatened to 'rape her in her mouth.'

It may sound naive but I felt I had to 'rescue' her. I registered my credit card and paid to go 'private.' Then it was me and her alone and all the other text stopped. Silence descended for a moment and she gazed into the screen. I felt sure she could see me ... somehow. I asked her questions, made general talk. I tried to explain that I just wanted to give her a break, but when the counter reached 40 minutes she started feeling guilty and gave me a 'performance' anyway. I told her nothing too heavy. She stroked her pussy. We chatted till my credit ran out as shreds of damp tissue dried and stuck to my keyboard. That night all I could think about was her in that room. Those sick people making demands of her. What kind of man wants to see a woman screw a cactus?

I was online the next morning as early as possible. She seemed pleased to see me and immediately went to private. It transpired that a sex performance was required at some time in our chat regardless. So, as the days and weeks passed I just asked her to use whatever she used at home and most enjoyed. Turned out to be a 'rabbit' vibrator. Like from 'Sex in the City.' She said that worked for her every time, even with the circumstances. Obviously, I found out more about her. As she grew to trust me she took my email and we began writing privately. Long messages about her thoughts, her work, her life. Soon we began calling each other. Somewhere there I fell in love. She said she thought she did too. That she felt great affection for me; that she liked the photos and the video I sent her; that when she performed for me in the chat it was almost like making love ... .

A little later she decided to leave. She had saved up enough money and would be coming out to see me. We would spend some time together and go from there. I made up the spare room for her. You may think that funny after I had seen all her intimacy; every inch of her body. But it didn't seem funny to me. It was the way I felt.

We decided we should spend her last day online together; almost like a little celebration really, of where we'd first met and what had come to be. How genuinely good things could come from the most unlikeliest circumstances. We went private straightaway, were chatting about when her flight landed, what we had planned. She gave me one final performance; using the rabbit vibrator on herself in all sorts of positions: she came doggy-style, her arse facing the screen ... .

It was then that the curtains behind her suddenly opened; billowing out obscuring the cams line of sight. She turned and I saw her scream. Then I saw ... *him*: a large, lumbering figure dressed all in black, a hood on his head, eye holes cut out in jagged, ragged slits. The screen froze and began to pixellate. Shouting, I tried to make sense of the jumble, but it was a sick jigsaw of frenzied colour; pieces of her, pieces of him, colliding in twisted juxtaposition. I could make out nothing. I typed and typed and typed furiously but there was no reply ... .

When I refreshed the screen, I was taken back to the menu and she was gone. I emailed the company but received no reply. I tried her private email but received a message the account was no longer in use. I rung her mobile phone but it had been disconnected .... The next day, another girl had taken her place on the menu screen. She was dark but her eyes were different; they were blank and lifeless. I called the police but it was a 'foreign matter' and it seemed there was little they could do and I knew they never took me seriously. A man, split from his girlfriend who falls in love with a web cam girl? Once they found out I was taking a course of antidepressants it was even worse. They concluded me deluded and could find no records of this 'particular sex-worker.' The employer had denied she had ever existed. But I know she *did*. I know she was real, I remember.

I saw something beautiful in her.

Written by A.D.Hitchin, 2009.

FOR REASONS UNKNOWN

By

Richard Kovitch

The boy's blood, opaque and viscid, trickled across the tarmac. A dark red cocktail of white and red cells, platelets and plasma, DNA and life itself, all now flowing into the gutter. Bone shards from where the skull had splintered drifted in the red sea like miniature life rafts. Compound fractures burst from both torso and limbs like crooked branches hewn of pinkish-white bone. Where the osseous tissue had split it revealed the deep red within, the medullary membrane and the marrow both now exposed to the watching crowd. Both compact and cancellous tissue had irretrievably broken down; an entire lifetime eradicated in a fragment of a second. The boy's heart was finally liberated from keeping him alive, its four chambers reduced to useless meat. The still morning air hung heavy. Everything had ceased.

The attending police officers would later speculate how long the boy had been alive after he had stepped from the car park roof and started to fall. Estimates varied from 1 second to 2.5 seconds. Because nobody could agree how long the body had been in the air specific calculations proved impossible. *32 feet is the acceleration to gravity but would that play a factor in a drop of only 4 storeys?* The only fact they could agree on, with a dark chuckle, was that whatever velocity had been reached during the fall, it was certainly terminal.

Indeed, when the body hit the street the impact was so intense it caused the skin to split, the boy's clothes now hanging from his teenage frame like bloody rags. *How many bruises were caused by the drop and how many predated it?* Nobody in the crowd cared as they fixed upon his pale teenage flesh. Sudoriferous glands lay covered in blood and dirt, wrists arched back against themselves causing the midcarpal joints to shatter. Arteries had burst upon impact, the cells had stopped living, both ontogeny and phylogeny had ceased. The somatic cells would build no more tissue. The germinal cells that were deigned to create life were dead.

Yet the boy's eyes remained wide open. They stared back at the watching crowd, accusing and desperate, still haunted by the life they had been forced to witness and the violent nature of its end. The retinas had dislodged on impact, organs of sight reduced to nothing, the crystalline lens bloodshot and useless. *Were the last moments of his life trapped in the pupil's epicentre?* It was futile to speculate, otherworldly and unanswerable.

The impact itself had silenced the crowd. In the hour before he jumped it had been rowdy, jeering and taunting him from the moment his ghostly silhouette appeared against the sky line. Humans do not need much encouragement to witness death. Instinctively they look, slowing down at road accidents to rubber neck, the evening television shows packed with entertaining fictional deaths. *Who can truly act with indifference towards something from which they cannot escape yet about which they have scant information?* And as soon as death is sensed the sympathetic nervous system pulses with epinephrine and focuses the attention, enteric nervous energy ripping through the body to activate a 'fight or flight' response that in this instance froze the crowd collectively to the spot. Walking away would have been impossible. It would have been against nature.

The crowd's sadism was harder to understand. Cat calls and gestures abounded as vocal chords trembled with cries of *"Jump"* and *"Do it."* When the suicide looked down he would have seen a sea of faces swirling beneath baying for his blood. Later it was revealed mobile phones had captured the moment of the fall, to be looped back as pixels in cyberspace. Police arrested some of the kids who had filmed the images, but they could find no breach of the law with which to charge them. What was certain was every doubt the jumper had about humanity, every charge of coldness and indifference he had made against the world was expressed by the mob gathered beneath him at the moment of his death.

The dead body was photographed then covered in a white blanket that stained red immediately. When forensics had finished their report the remains were loaded into an ambulance. The tarmac was cleaned quickly. Sawdust absorbed the blood, while the physical remnants were scraped into yellow, plastic bags. His teeth had bounced far and wide, some falling at the feet of the crowd. Not all them were recovered. An autopsy was conducted later that day, but it was impossible to locate an explanation for the boy's state of mind from his physical remains alone. Any evidence of abuse had mangled with the torture his body had undergone when it slammed into the tarmac. No explanatory note was ever found and it was days before his identity was revealed, a footnote in the newspaper quickly forgotten.

I cannot recall his name either. I abandoned the crowd soon after the boy had fallen, disgusted at the blood lust of the onlookers. Yet to this day when I walk past that same spot I glance up and see him, frozen in the air, an angel tumbling from heaven, wings broken, caught in a freefall. *On the way down what did he feel? Had he simply exchanged one sequence of events beyond his control for another?* Such questions never find answers. I remain convinced a dark shadow haunts the road where he fell, this murky outline his only legacy, but I may be imagining it. I doubt very much anyone else passing through gives it even a seconds thought.

Richard Kovitch © 2009

Some Kind of Stranger III

Christopher Nosnibor

He was young, free and newly single, and he was cruising now, ready to make up for lost time, ready for action. It wasn't his natural state, but what the hell: for too long he had allowed himself to be pushed around, dictated to, to allow others to choose the course of his life. Girlfriends, bosses, his mother... well not tonight. Tonight he was going to party like it was 1999. Not that he had actually partied back in '99... but still, now he was free of Abigail, rather than mourn 18 wasted months with that psycho bitch, he was going to drink, drink, drink and be ill, and he was going to paint the town red.

He had called his friend Rob up, and Rob had reluctantly agreed to go clubbing. Jim and Bob were strangely matched friends. Rob suspected it was as much out of habit as anything, having been friends through school. Jim never gave it any thought. He didn't have all that many friends and had spent the last few years concentrating on his career rather than his social network. Like James, Robert was approaching 30 and had been out of the social scene for a long time, but that was entirely his choice. Whereas Jim was cautious but yearned to experience life, Rob was simply misanthropic, and was as predisposed to dismiss virtually everything as 'shit' now as he had been a decade ago.

"Man, I hate clubs," he had moaned when James had told him the evening's plan. "They're crap... the beer's piss, the music's shit and it's wall-to-wall twats, of both sexes."

But James had insisted that his friend join him in this time of crisis. Without analysing his own shoddy motives, he wanted to feel young and vibrant again, and to check out the totty that had been off-limits for the year and a half he had been with Abbie, and for the year or five before that while he had concentrated on his career. He wanted to feel the danger. Was it too late? Was it really what he wanted? He felt prickly, awkward and uncomfortable, but it's what people did after a break-up.

The night was young, the moon was mellow and James felt as though he could kiss the sky. Quite uncharacteristically, he spoke loudy, brashly and volubly. In the queue for the club, the two men surveyed the scene and saw things very differently. Or were the sights they saw so very different?

Rob scowled. Although now into March, Spring had not yet sprung, and Winter's icy claw scraped the sky. He scanned those around him. Most were much younger than he and his mate; others were, like him, clearly old enough to know better. Muttons, bingo wings a-flapping, barely dressed as lamb, and old letches in shiny shirts and polished shoes, eyeing up the girls they were old enough to have fathered. As he saw it, the 'social lives' upon which so much emphasis is placed by so many are merely a façade, torture dressed as fun, a rolling compulsion, unwilling to miss out on something – however trivial – or to be seen to be a lightweight, unable to take the pace. Sure, one more round… what'll it be, then?

James wasn't sure what he was doing. The three pints he had downed in the pub beforehand served as a mild anaesthetic, but he felt out of place and old, very fucking old. While checking out his prospects – and there were many – he found himself, inevitably, reflecting not only on his now-defunct relationship with Abigail, but also his other past failed relationships.

Back in school, despite being as shy and awkward as any teenager, he had faired pretty well, and while he'd never really appreciated being considered 'cute,' given his lack of looks or sporting prowess, he'd not complained. In the first years of secondary school, he had lacked the confidence to speak to any girls, his experience being restricted to a handful of now long-forgotten private crushes. But entering the fourth year and his GCSEs, something had changed and the floodgates opened. First, there had been Lisa. They had been fifteen. The relationship had probably only lasted a couple of months, and their physical exchanges amounted to little more than a few nervous fumbles, but she had been the first girl he had seen topless and whom he had touched, and the excitement... even now, though it was half a lifetime away, the thought of her and the newness of the experience made him stiffen. There had been others shortly after; Megan had been uptight and bossy and he'd not got very far – or lasted very long – with her, and there had been his on/off thing with Hannah. She'd blown hot and cold and so had he, and sometimes he had enjoyed the fact she was wanting to push things on but others... despite the fact that she had proportionally large breasts, her nipples were remarkably small, masculine, and despite the fact they had never had full sex, she had remained a wank-fantasy of his for years. He had lost his virginity to some tubby slapper friend-of-a-friend's while at university. Her name was Jo, and although the relationship had been brief and imploded in a splatter of acrimony after about three months, it had been a steep learning curve for him in sexual terms. The intervening years had been more sedate – a couple of girls he had dated casually whose names he now forgot, two years with Amy, and then, last but not least, Abigail.

How she had annoyed him! Initially he had been compliant with her domineering, manipulative ways, had gone along with everything she had wanted, but still she had demanded more. He wanted the finer things in life: a decent job, a nice car, a biggish house, and an attractive girl on his arm. And why not? His ambition in life was success, and he wanted the world to look at him and know he was a successful man. But he had limits as to how much we would tolerate to achieve all of these things, and attractive as Abi was, she was high maintenance. But even when she was at her most unreasonable, James had made every effort to avoid confrontation. The long hours tinkering in the garage to get some peace...

But he didn't want to think about it too much. No, he had his eyes on a new prize now. He was like a kid in a sweet shop, his pupils were flitting like Saturday's bonus ball across the shiny delights all around him.

"So it was you that ended it then?"

"Yeah, I just said 'fuck it' and called it a day," Jim lied with a bucketful of faux bravado. It was hard to tell whom he was trying to convince.

"So has she moved out, or...?" Rob quizzed.

"Um, no," Jim hovered. "I'm sleeping on the sofa at the moment. But she's away visiting her family this weekend."

Once inside the club, Jim and Rob got stuck into some hyperchilled gaseous pisswater: Jim because he wanted to forget life, Rob because he wanted to forget where he was. The music pulsated, and before long they were drunk and the dancefloor was really beginning to heat up. The lighting was poor, and the more Rob drank, the stranger uglier everyone looked to him. But Jim was on fire. The bodies twisting serpentine, glistening with perspiration, and the eyes that shine... He wanted it like in the movies, wanted it like in the porn he had downloaded on those rare evenings when Abigail had gone out, or away to visit her family for the weekend. Yes, life is short and love is always over in the morning, but rationale, rhyme and reason pale beside a single kiss...

How would it turn out? Something cherry ripe and novel, or something miserable, something faded, something crushed, or something old like any jilted roadside blonde?

James wasn't thinking beyond what he wanted as he turned his drunken leer on some size 8 bottle-blonde in an impossibly short skirt and dangerously low-cut halter-neck top. He liked the way she put her hands up in the air. He liked the way she shook her hair. He liked the way she moved. Her Sartorious were well-defined as she moved her toned thighs and gyrated her pelvis in time with the pulsating rhythms and pounding beats.

His parotid, submaxillary and sublingual salivary glands went into overdrive, pouring their juices into the cavity of his mouth, running thick inside his cheeks. He was feeling courageous. He began by dancing close, throwing moves and postures. In time with one another, they were slaves to the DJ, out of control... Soon he was talking to her. She was laughing. Yes! He was really doing this! His cock was on fire. He wanted to grab her by the hair and throw her against the wall... but pace is the trick, he thought, and instead placed a hand on her naked thigh as he went to whisper in her ear...

Rob hung back by the bar, a scowl fixed on his face as he slung back bottle after bottle. The Stella, in combination with the atrocious music that shook him to the very core with its relentless throbbing basslines, was giving him a headache. He was nowhere near drunk enough to be into this. Rob was a musical obscurist, and of all the music he detested, dance, especially mainstream dance, had to rank as his most loathed style of music. And even more than he abhorred dance music, he abhorred the kind of people who listened to it through choice. As he watched on, Jim's behaviour increasingly baffled him. Clearly, he was drunk, and clearly, he was in some sort of shock after breaking up with Abigail. But to see him glassy-eyed and dancing like he had a wet finger in a live socket, practically molesting the girl he had 'met' not ten minutes earlier in full public view... it wasn't good form, and it wasn't the James he knew. James wasn't the James he knew either: he was really letting go for perhaps the first time in his life and he was loving it.

This is it! This is what I've been missing out on!

"...you *dare* go near my bird, eh? *EH?*"

James was suddenly propelled backwards a few paces. Some burly bloke with short-cropped hair and bloodshot brown eyes was in his face. He was suddenly mute, then spluttering, inchoate.

"You want some, eh?" Hands were on him now. In a whirl of alcohol fuelled disorientation, he was moving, and within moments was on the street facing the hard-looking guy who was slender but wiry.

The realisation that he had gone too far hit at the same instant that the thug's fist met with his face. He deflated like a balloon that had been punctured with a pin as he felt his Pyramidalis Nasi collapse under the force of the blow. Plasma and platelets exploded from busted corpuscles and ran in rivulets from his nostrils, down over his upper lip and into his mouth. He could taste the floor as the meathead's smart patent leather shoe connected with his kidneys. A series of kicks to his abdomen and thorax in quick succession, culminating with a boot to the solar plexus resulted in an involuntary regurgitation of the evening's beverages, and the bastard wasn't done yet.

Rob emerged from the venue now, and the cold air hit him like a slap in the face but he could only look on as his friend's blood flowed.

An alternative version of 'Some Kind of Stranger' appeared in the Winter 2008 edition of *Geeek Magazine*.

Clinical, Brutal....

THE PROTOCOL OF SURFACE NOISE

Lee Kwo

Wrack the lever of infernal xxovum combustions noise
Bound eyes of the sleepwalker anal-logical victim
a contusional nudity of neural fallacious impotence
obsessive vandalism under liquid voltage horizon
deceptive in its gravity she weeps tears of coded silence

Servo severed vascular GroinEngine without mor[t]al inference
Lost in the beauty of indifference to memories short circuit
fear flux ruined thin spectacle plenitudes of ironical paradox
insolence of vice in her disease she peaked with unction

Clutch of obscure pain pinned down oral perversity
to lie as inconsistency of wreckless haptic speech
versus vicious thoughts of XXPhallic adornment
Auto Pilot engages remote control dissonance
as retinal images leave eyes prosthetic turmoil

Talk about a future in which we fail to exist Vox say
Push the limit to reclining spatial planes of nubile sanctity
hinges of saliva perceived life within her Sapphic cunt
The autopsied corpse of Absurdinas final moment of desire
where hatred finds its means of production and exchange
Transparent objects watch electrons sordid glow coalesque
while reality moves in advance of your violated arrival

Cool memories of past time falling apart prohibitively tranquillized
under subvocal dimensions of contagious congenital flaws

Over exposure to the transitional referent I desire
Chernuka pornstar Veydra Kulak drinks Bombay Sapphire
on her empty balcony replay Black Box flight recorder
salvaged from wreckage of her stellar Pineal Gland

Reciprocity of open space continuum mutation frequencies
Gunships open fire on Assassins in Desert of Nagazaki
Pain threshold increases on a scale of one to one
Dead rodent visceral spark hits celestial speed of light

Profane noise of unmediated Laws atonality
sleepless eyes that have never seen mans fear
within delirium of universes instants velocity kills
new wave of expulsion from coupling morbid fixity
incites slowly moving seconds of chemical induced time

The sole witness to this anarchic velocity to sleep
Coded flows of abstract dialogue under psychotic complicity
Some suicide others bleed to death some sleep the sacred death
within a network programmed to kill extinctions glory
what matters is the abyss the ocean of annihilation

You dismantle each strategy keep intimate things tenuous
threaten to vacate prosthetic limbic radiance
ambient channels of sound wear thin like threads

Clinical, Brutal....

The hostile craving for annunciation of insomnia SKz

Space ignites and leaves its atomic weapons on alert
Impulsive passions stalled on nostalgic stationary voyage
The blocked insertion of ejected articulation to interrupt
Just a function of the drained vortex of media fatigue

Without a jagged deception the dream of power stalls
Across fluid neon signs disrupted flux narcissistic horror
this circulating predatory spirit of surveillance scans the coldness
where death has no advocates and no memory only sleep
Flaps through depth of space corroded numeral of visibility
attacks the superstition of the self as existential shit mess

For more information run scan of distress mode narcolepsy
shadows in auto erotic zone give birth astride a grave
Moments broken by static violation hit full metal bondage
At last yr failure has no exits thru terminal excrescence

Noise the purest burst of transient materiality
Density of notes under interrogation of self induced hynosis
The puzzle of yr implication in corrosive deciet
mechanistic paradigm of a manic bullet in motion

Death albatross drowned in perverse explication of cranial scar
a random drift a delirious passivity under distorted sublation
detours of wasted energy to narcotic fadeout of post literate
Data accidents in hysterical progress of silent dread conspiracy

Incision of fatality attacks satiric impulse devoid of suspicion
where forbidden dreams and memories are exposed
Screen matrix neuron phillia plague of dog-matic razOr Gril
Savage the warning sighs to imagine data trash on alert mode
noise becomes a point of departure rather than arrival
the sonic as unmediated vector achieves tears of coded silence

Clinical, Brutal....

Test Broadcast from the Zone of Occupation/

Lee Kwo

Addiction to Codeine Wars bruised and penetrated fuk low level probe
RomRok without mortal influence hits the worn out spike tract limits
Lost in the beauty of indifference to velocity of ganglion ligatures
The lies as inconsistency of wreckless speech causes bivalves to open
stigmata oil floods cellular matrix under visceral techno beast spasm
Versus plots of vicious thought of molecules in a technology of
reflection
lubricates glass muscle of modalities under alterity of solar anus
an equal pain whether she speaks or remains silent returns or leaves with
sorrow
Auto Pilot engages remote control transit districts to the front line
Retinal images leave prosthetic turmoil ball bearing crack on terminal
glaze
an absolute dereliction virtual nucleus of bruised wreck/
Talk about the future in which we exist under hypodermic incisions
Push the limit to reclining nude of sanctity florescent tubes hiss/
The autopsied corpse of a subjects final moment has no passion
to transgress SexEngine no longer exists fear has replaced its perversity
Ignited by the rancour of diseased organs tracer void of drug induced
torpor
leaves imprints of War Machine dust of word blinds the heroism of
psychosis
wired to the outside world thru which we inscribe ourselves
Hatred finds its means of production and exchange within our own flesh

Transparent objects under surveillance watch electrons sordid glow

Reality moves ahead in advance of your arrival as fractured occipital lobe

Cool memories of past time falling apart stare comatose at

Subvocal dimensions of hidden appearances thin light crackle

Long before the invention of insomnia the boundless dreams of the sleepwalker

loops the antenna embryo infiltrates the blunt corpse

Over exposure to the transitional referent visceral engine logic

Reciprocity of open space continuum addiction to irony of dialectics

Gunships open fire on assassins in Desert of Nagazaki RomRok suicide

Pain threshold increases on a scale of one to one on plasma red horizon

Dead rodent visceral spark hits speed of light consensual hellucination

Profane noise of unmediated Law hijacked terror of bodily abjection

Equal to those with amputated limbs there are no celibate autopsies on Atomic beach

A whole new wave of expulsion as passions are mere fatalities

Slowly moving seconds of chemical induced time erode viral tissue

the sole witness to this anarchic velocity excites razor slash Gashgril

Coded flows of abstracted dead ends blitz of magnesium detritus

Some suicide others bleed to death as logic proliferates surface noise

Under a network programmed to kill extinction paranoiac devices inserted

Execution of the tattered maps plot the duration of erections

The hostile craving for annunciation aberrations distorted by artifice

Space ignites and leaves its weapons narcotic sleep deprived eyelids

Impulsive passions stalled on zero do not need to be mourned

The blocked insertion of ejected articulation strangles avatar identity

Clinical, Brutal....

Just a function of the drained vortex to infiltrate and resurrect

Without a jagged deception the dream of power stalls a state of rupture

Across fluid neon signs disrupted flux under propellor thrust wind hits
target

and ExtremaDura is so beautiful in her moments of captivity

This circulated predatory spirit runs transit districts to the front line

Flaps through dead water on rogue male XX phallic galvanised war
engines deceitful panic

For more information run scan of distress signal from loves distant shore

Shadows in the auto zerotic zone the blood of the Nomad is on yr hands

Moments broken by static violation we are at war with the assassins

At last a failure has no exits a nuclear desire for despair

The purest burst of transient materiality points of torso impact

Density of notes under interrogation a comet of frail solitude

The puzzle of yr implication killing thought after a sense of direction

Love albatross coding the flow where technical machines evade memory

Vacant lot backwash of foetal distortion the bachelors severed eroticism

Dead fish scream to cultural enigmatic unreality becomes tangible

Data accidents in hysterical progress shot dead in the streets

Incision of induced fatality attack where all technology is suspicious

Screen matrix neuron phillia plague a proto text plotting co-ordinates

Savage the warning sighs to imagine yr extinction under mortal wound

A paradox without dilemma the inside gives itself up to Endcodes

Exhumation of the Post Human Sublation

Lee Kwo

Sun exfoliates as a depth tide for extinction
a post verbal interruption of intervals devours the underworld
[katabasis]
Icarus crashed from the latent radiance of solar voyage thru vanity
A state of ungestalt is a question of depth
or resonance with the machinic abyss / the deformed interference of
excess static clichés of subversion under exposed junk Apparatus
Wide eyed to glyphs the logic of the negative the among systems of
passages of collapsing affinities nothing to be said tearing to shred the
word
It was there from the start the masculine stuttering the feminine
pleasures erosion of desire and macht [puissance] power under erasure
a betrayal of the self into phillia of descents and wastage of enmity
Role plays avatars accomplices comrades infiltrations of the interval
destiny of joy speaks from with in cold hard closed texts
Expression without consciousness who can we be then?/
Memory traces enmeshing a capacity for dreaming
darkness is the chromatic gradient of reality in depth/death
the anonymous map of becoming woman will have its ecstasy
culture jamming in its purest form
the shadow of the writer as after image
illuminated by the combustion of a destitute epoch
The madman speaks the language of the fantastic and passionate
there is a secret delirium underlying the chaotics of immateriality/

Clinical, Brutal....

delivered of all the excess of dementia

The wall of sounds contains/refrains the Garden

The House is thinking an obscenity of exhuming dissonances

there are twists of darkness on the event horizon

The NOW is not lost but becomes a mutant with

anonymous rates of acceleration impossible to be disentangled

there is pleasure in hysteria/a transgression/a loss of control

that sets the epidemic of words into flows and intensities

there is pleasure in a abstraction of context

An evaporation of the regime of signs frenzied lines of vortices

The shadow of the Writer under erasure is a precondition

for discussing this detour into hysteria which leaves its masks

excess of evidence for the pack to trace/

and so to erase the symbolic under the law of the father

replacing it with what/where/ NOW/

the exhumation of the Post Human the implosion of the phallic

Caveat Pre-emptor

S F Grimm

"Fuck off you bastard!" I shouted with a smile into the phone.

I picked up my mug of tea off the desk, spilling some over a half-read copy of yesterday's Yorkshire Post. "Yeah, fuck him – he's a pisshead anyway. They'll serve the papers whatever we do - and then we'll deal with it." I stood up from my desk and used my foot to push the bit of folded cardboard back under the battered filing cabinet that was keeping it upright. "Listen, when are you next up our way?" I asked, lighting up a Benson and Hedges Superking. "I'll buy you a pint – I think you need it..... Yeah...Well, there's nothing we can do about it now is there..... No, fuck it.... Listen, I can hardly hear you now, mate – give me a bell when you're back in the office, yeah?"

There was a knock at my office door. It opened and my secretary did her fidgety hand waving gesture that meant she was asking if it was alright to let someone in. I nodded. Behind her was a girl – I guessed the one who I said I'd agree to meet up with yesterday.

I stubbed out my half-smoked cigarette. "Look, I've got to go now... Ha! Like you lost to me last time?.. Yeah ok. Cheers."

The girl sat on the chair opposite my desk. She looked no more than 18. Her pink bomber jacket was immaculate and her white jeans were still tight, but reverse-faded to a bluish grey. Her white Reebok trainers were a little scuffed. What I really drew my attention were her hands. Her fingernails were really, really badly bitten. Really fucking disgusting. *Really* fucking disgusting. They were almost completely gone on a few fingers – just three or four millimetres of nail bed and then rough little bits of shredded dead skin like they'd been superglued back over an open wound. She took the holdall she came in with and pushed it under her chair. I couldn't really tell what colour or make because it looked like it had been taken out of a burning skip.

Her hands were a greasy sort of dirty too. Grainy – like she'd been fixing a car the day before. She was fairly pale and had frizzy light brown hair. Frizzy from being fucked, not from being curly. It was in a ponytail, scraped back so tight I could almost see her hair ping out of their follicles under the sheer pressure.

She wasn't pretty... But she weren't ugly either. Her features were all in proportion, but the angles were rounded off in the wrong places. She sat with her right foot tucked under her left thigh, playing with her mobile phone. It was an old baby blue Nokia 8310 – too old to have much on it to play with. I could tell she wasn't nervous or shy – just another waste of breath. She made my shitty little office look even worse than it did normally. She looked me in the eye when I spoke.

I sat back down and checked her name again on the papers. "Miss Faddon, right?"

"I want you to investigate a murder for me," she said. Straight out.

Her accent was local, like mine. She spoke to me like she was buying ten Mayfair from the local corner shop. I made some immediate, but conscious assumptions: probably left school at 16. No qualifications. Probably got into petty theft, had the occasional fight, bunked off, made trouble – the absolute usual. She probably has a couple of children from different fathers. Probably on the dole. Probably takes drugs. Most of her boyfriends have probably been in prison. Likely there's been some domestic violence at some point in her life. Probably lives somewhere like the Granville Terraces.

She probably thinks she's assertive. But I bet she's just thick as shite.

I belittled her. To be fair I was still on auto-pilot though. It was just gone nine in the morning, and just before the call from Paul the Sparky earlier, I had a right barney on the phone with some arsehole solicitor who thinks he's clever, representing a client who thinks he's right.

I replied, "Er, you know what? The police usually like to take care of that sort of thing. So I'd say it's best if..."

"Obviously, I can't go to the police, can I?" she interrupted. She spoke to me like I was a fucking idiot. What she really meant was "Obviously, I can't go to the police, can I? *You twat.*"

Fine, I thought, *Whatever. Just wrap it up straight away and get the rest of the day over.* Stupid cow.

I looked down at my own hands for a second. They looked *old.* I felt thirsty. I needed to drink something. Something, anything – a glass of water, a can of Coke, a rum and Coke. A can of Tenants and a good fucking punch-up.

Back to the cow at hand. "Ok, so you can't go to the police. Why not?" I asked.

"I can't tell you," she said, in a tone that indicated that she felt it sufficient that I should drop that particular line of enquiry there and then. She clearly thought she knew my job far better than I did, and what she's told me is all she thinks I need to know.

I looked down, talking to her without bothering to make eye contact anymore. I started filling in the interview sheet from bottom up – starting with the words 'Taken case no further'.

I just asked the questions as they came to me. I didn't need a headache brought on from her being any more difficult than I expected her to be, so I just thought I'd go through the motions. "Fair enough. So, er... who's this murder victim then?" Professional. Cool. Calm. Cow.

"I am," she said.

"You what?" I laughed – just the breath in a laugh, just a quarter of a chuckle. But I laughed.

She curled her lip. "It's me."

There was a smacking sound against the far wall of my office. From the outside 'Ow you cunt!' came a young voice.

"I'm dead serious," she said.

"Someone wants you dead?" I asked. I looked at her again. *What's she playing at?* I thought.

She rolled her eyes and put her phone in her pocket. She answered like she'd been caught shoplifting, and the best form of defence she could come up with at the time was childish sarcasm. "Yes." She spoke rhythmically to underscore how thick I was to not get what she was saying – dum de dum de dum: "Someone wants me dead."

What the fuck? What is she talking about? I thought.

"And you want me to... protect you or something?"

"No. I don't want protection. I wouldn't go to you for protection." *Fair enough* I think. There are people in her neck of the woods far better at that than me. "Then what do you want?" I asked.

"I want you to find out who killed me." The silent 'you stupid twat' still lingered with each sentence she spoke.

"You mean who's going to kill you." To be honest I don't know why I said that. I don't know what I was doing by then – correcting her grammar? What am, I her fucking English teacher?

She spoke in a tone now that was pretty matter of fact. "No. I'm going to be murdered. I would like you find out who did it."

I kind of felt sorry for her. Girls like this just bring it out of you. Pathetic, horrible losers – but really just children at the end of the day. "Are you sure you're going to be murdered?" I asked.

"Yes I'm fucking sure." She closed her eyes, shook her head, and made a click-clicking sound from the moisture between her lips as she opened her mouth to breathe in. The noise sounded remarkably like she was very quietly saying the word 'dickhead.'

"Look I don't know what you're playing at, but I'm not in the mood for being bullshitted. It's probably better if you fuck the fuck out." I started to stand.

"Fuck the fuck out?" she mocked. She held on tight to the arms of the chair. She raised her voice. The outer corner of her eyes dropped and her nostrils narrowed. She barely moved her lips. "I'm fucking serious. Just hear me out first, before you fucking boot me out, will you? I've got money. You're an investigator, I've got something I want you to investigate. What's the fucking problem?"

I couldn't work her out. I thought about it for a second: *Is this even quarter true? No, she's clearly full of shit.... I think.* I decided to see the meeting out to its conclusion and then say no as firmly as need be.

"Ok. So who wants you dead?" I asked.

"If I knew that, I wouldn't be here, would I? Fuck's sake."

"Fine. So is there not like, you know – no way to stop them doing it? Hiding or whatever, to stop them from killing you?"

"No. I'll be murdered. I'll be murdered very soon. I don't want you to do – or to worry about – anything else. Just find out who did it." She pretty much ordered me.

Oh fuck this, I thought. *This girl's making you look like a dick, and you've got better things to do with your time.*

"First of all, you're not ordering a fucking Chinky, you're asking me to investigate a murder without the police's involvement. And secondly, seem pretty fucking relaxed, but then you're telling me... Well, you're saying to me you're going to actually die, and don't seem in the grand scheme of things particularly bothered by it."

"No. You're wrong. Of course I'm fucking bothered. But I don't..." She breathed out a sigh you make just before you start to cry. "There's nothing I can do other than come here and..." She paused again, breathed in hard. "Christ, it should be pretty obvious by the fucking fact that I'm fucking talking to you right fucking now that there's nothing I can do about it, shouldn't it?"

"Ok. I'm sorry," I said. Then, for the first time since she walked in, it seriously – *seriously* – dawned on me that it was possible that she might have been telling the truth. That someone really was going to kill her.

"So, why do they want you dead?"

"I can't tell you."

"How do you know you'll be murdered then?"

Her eyes momentarily narrowed – she really thought I was an idiot. A slight curl of her lip again. "I can't tell you that either, can I?"

"Ok. Do you know when they'll do it?" *What a fucking bizarre question I'm asking*, I thought.

"Tomorrow morning."

"Can you tell me, you know – how they'll do it?"

"Yes. I can tell you that. I'll be found dead from a sleeping pill overdose in a hotel room that I'll rent in town later today."

Jesus. That was pretty specific. "This is the fucking weirdest conversation I've had in a long time," I say to her. I reach around in my empty pockets for the cigarettes I'd left on the desk.

"How do you know?" I ask. "How do you know when you're going to die? How do you *how* you're going to die? That is really, really strange. You got to admit."

"I can't tell you," she says. "What I've told you is all I can tell you. You can keep asking me questions, but I'll just say either I don't know or I can't tell you."

"But why don't you just run away?"

"I can't. I don't have... I just can't." I looked at her. *Fucking hell*, I thought, *Whatever is going on, I don't think she's just here to wind me up.*

"Why don't you just not rent the hotel room?"

"I can't."

"Why not go to the police?"

"I fucking told you that! I can't!" She snapped. She pulled her legs in tighter and pulled at her sleeves.

"Alright, alright – yeah yeah yeah yeah. Sorry. I know I already asked that." I stood up to stretch my legs, then sit on the side of the desk, shifting my weight so it didn't buckle from being so old and shit. "OK, how about I just don't let you out of this room?"

Clinical, Brutal....

"You won't be able to."

"What about help from, I don't know – family, friends, loved ones?"

She looked me in the eyes. I could sense that I was the only person who she'd talked to about this. And that she really did want my help.

"I can't tell you any more than I've already told you, but you're not..." She scratched her arms. "Look, what you're suggesting, they're good ideas and that. But they won't help me. Believe me – it won't help. There's nothing I can do, there's nothing you can do, there's nothing anyone can do."

"Fair enough." I pull the blind on the window to the side and see a little Jack Russell pissing against the front wheel of my Vauxhall Corsa.

"There's something that doesn't quite work though," I said to her, looking up. "If whoever wants to kill you can go to all this trouble to make it impossible to stop that from happening, what makes you think that the moment someone starts poking their nose around after, that person wouldn't be next on the list?"

"You're wrong. It's not how it works. You don't understand."

"Clearly." I glance at my watch. 10 minutes of my life wasted on this shit. "Look, Ms Faddon, please don't take offence. But here's what I think. There are three variables: a) your general level of sanity b) Whether you're trying to frame someone for your own murder or some other such stupid Jeremy Kyle Show bollocks. And c) if you're naive enough to think that I'd get involved in this crap in some way, some shape, or some fucking dick-arsed form. I don't honestly give a fuck about a or b, but I can tell you straight as a fucking crystal clear die, I am not the right person to engage in this kind of work. I don't know what you think I do, but it is certainly not this. So as I said earlier, I think you should you 'fuck the fuck out.'"

"I'll pay you ten times what you normally charge."

Ok, that hadn't come up yet. I looked at the ceiling, squinting with my tongue pressed against the side my lips. I made up figures on the spot. "That would work out to be..." I looked through the cracks in the blind again – that fucking dog was crapping right in front of my car now. "That's... £4,500 a day, plus expenses. And expenses covers all food, all travel costs and all lodgings. And that includes room service too." That should do it, I thought.

"Fine - I'll pay it."

"Er... I'll be honest, I was taking shit. I'm not doing it."

There was a flicker of something that showed in her face for the first time she'd walked in. "Look, no offence to you Mr Miller, but looking at the state of your office, not to mention the people I got your number from; I don't really think you're in any position to turn me down."

Fucking hell, I thought.

"I'll pay up-front, full whack." She said.

I breathe a sigh. "Jesus Christ."

To her that obviously meant I'll take the job: "I have a time limit though."

"A what?"

She seemed almost businesslike now. "You'll have 14 days from tomorrow morning. What's 14 lots of 4,500?"

"Err... sixty three grand."

Clinical, Brutal....

Did she see the pound signs roll across my eyes? "I'll give you sixty three grand plus an extra ten thousand pounds for expenses."

My mobile beeped. I snapped back to reality. "Huh, you have that in cash then do you?"

"I got a hundred grand in this bag with me now. You can keep the rest as if you find out who did it."

"And what do you expect me to do with the other...seventeen, sorry twenty seven grand if I don't?"

"I don't know... take it anyway? I don't know - give it charity if you want. I don't give a fuck."

I closed my eyes. "Ok...If I were to...Supposing that..." Fucking hell, I thought – what am fucking doing?

"What happens in 14 days time?"

"Something will happen that will make finding out who did it impossible. And then it wouldn't matter anymore anyway."

Oh fuck this, I thought. End this once and for all. "Ok, let's wrap this up. Ms Faddon, that is a very good offer. But, I'm afraid that again I am going to have to decline. We do mostly small business stuff - fraud, embezzlement etc. 'White collar crime', that sort of thing. And I'm also afraid that this conversation, should you actually be found dead any time soon - not that I believe a fucking word you've said - is going to make me look pretty fucking suspicious to the police. So, I'm going to ask my secretary to make a copy of the recording of the conversation we've just had... Yes, I am recording this right now. It's clearly stated on the form you signed before you came in. I'm then going to call a contact of mine at the local police station, let him know we've spoken, and that I've told you I don't want fuck all to do with you."

She pulls the holdall from under the chair. She opens the zipper. "Look, here it is. A hundred grand." It looked very much like a bag with one hundred thousand pounds in it.

"Fuck me. So who do I tell if I do find out who did it?"

"You don't need to worry about that. Just find them."

Clinical, Brutal....

Mr. Bones

David Mark Dannov

If you look
at man

without his skin
and see his skeleton
you'll notice he's not
much different
than most
animals
on the planet.

He has a backbone like a horse
and ribs
like a cat
and a skull
like any mammal
crawling
on all fours.

The similarity
interests me
on a basic
primal level.

Smart as we are—

    rocket ships,

    the knowledge of our own mortality,

    science, medicine, astronomy—

we really are

just bones

evolved

from the bowels

of the earth.

Clinical, Brutal....

The Soul Monster

David Mark Dannov

I sit here
on my couch
and look at the walls

     bored

     enough

     to kill.

What do we have to do
to liven up the night.

     Streets, cars, walls,
malls, restaurants—
everywhere we go
it seems
people are holding back
the fire blazing
in their bones.

     What else could it be

     but fear

     dominating

     their lives.

I'm disgusted
by the whole damn race.

I don't belong here.

I should be dancing
around a drum circle, naked,
with the rhythm of cannibals
            flickering
with the flames
of a bonfire.

Right now, I'd rather
eat worms,
      lick the skull of a dead man
            than sit here
like a civilized chimp
            feeling guilty
      for craving
        the taste
          of blood.

THE WILD HUNT

D M Mitchell

Night blotted out the heaven like the carapace of a huge shiny insect. Pickman hurtled along a river of panic on a red raft of his own pulsing, sugared blood. He could smell his nemesis behind him; - close now, moving relentlessly with the self assurance of a hangman's knot. His hunter had herded him to this place of inner-city desolation, away from his friends. The bastard knew what he was going to do, seemingly better than he did himself. Pickman was pissing-his-pants scared. This shouldn't be happening to him. He was a fucking artist! This would never have happened to Damien Hirst or Tracey Emin. If he could find a phone-box he should phone Saatchi and call in the 'anti-semitic' card!

Filtering in from the edges of his awareness, he became aware of another smell – a stale yellow stench like old people – like rotten wallpaper and the rancid stale-bread reek of death, ancient crusts moldering in a urinal. As he stood against the wall gulping the cold stinging air, his nostrils filled up with the odor, making him retch like an old wino after one bottle too many of White Lightning.

A terrible understanding dawned on him that this was really the end, snuffling around him like the shadow beast of his childhood – Shub Niggurath, the Great Swine Mother Of All Things come to eat his soul, digest his ka, and tear him into a thousand shrieking fragments, finally to absorb him back into her Womb of Darkness.

He was only a hundred and three but had seen so many things. How many mortals could say they'd seen the things that burrow beneath their safe little homes watching them at work and play, peering in at their windows at night? Some of the more sensitive of the clods would occasionally have caught a fleeting glimpse of the things that inhabited angled space where it intersected their own curved space.

Pickman had been past the Tomb Portal, beyond the Seventh Pylon, down the Twelve Thousand Steps and seen the long-dead feasting below with Britney, Madonna, Johnny Depp and the rest of the celebs. One day he would have been invited to join in, savouring the Holy Communion of Televised Immortality. It seemed so unfair that he'd now be cheated of this, unfair that he wouldn't even see the Black Man, and never get his OBE from Her Majesty the Fucking Queen for his services to Art.

The wall was wet and warm under his palms, like an aroused cunt. He found it strangely sensuous with the clarity bestowed only on the condemned. He gazed up at the sluggishly moving clouds, like clumps of dark matter on a great purple river. He hated London – it was too big and too full of mindless fools and the partially alive. London weaved an evil spell over its inhabitants, turning them into chittering, jabbering shells of things, with no will nor volition, whose every movement and action was little more than a habitual nervous twitch. Spiteful cold cerebral aberrations. Vampiric rigid things that resembled sticks …. or bones. Pickman wished that New York still existed. That was the place to be. Art had oozed out of that place like pus out of a syphilitic dick. The best you could hope for here was to be written into an Iain Sinclair novel. Ughhhh!!!

The gunshot took him by surprise, smashing a fist-sized hole in the brick wall near his head. Snapped back to full alertness, Pickman leaped the wall like a scalded cat, landing awkwardly and noisily in a cluster of rubbish bins on the other side. Blood trickled down his face from slivers of masonry. He hissed viciously, cursing himself. All his feral experience seemed to be deserting him. In a way, he couldn't help but admire this man who had appointed himself judge and executioner. Given the circumstances, he would have behaved exactly the same.

As he sprinted from the alley he collided awkwardly with a uniformed policeman (the new uniform – head to toe bondage rubber complete with pig mask and strap-on dildo), knocking him flying. A crowd of people outside a falafel stand nearby turned their way. Someone laughed. Pickman turned to run but the policeman ill-advisedly grabbed his trouser leg, pulling him off balance. Pickman hissed, spat like a mongoose, showing long, dripping hollow canines. The poor bastard's eyes widened in shock almost comically and, though he opened his mouth, no words came out – but he clung doggedly to Pickman's leg. Maybe he was paralysed with fear. No matter.

Pickman wriggled his fingers as though doing piano warm-up exercises, then thrust his claw into the man's abdomen, making a vertical incision from the ensiform cartilage to the pubes, then rending from the umbilicus, obliquely upwards and outwards to the outer surface of the chest as high as (he guessed) the low border of the fifth or sixth rib.

The man screamed like a cornered mink, as Pickman slashed again – midway between the umbilicus and pubes, transversely outwards to the anterior superior iliac spine, along the crest of the ileum as far as its posterior third. He took pride in his skills, his knowledge of the anatomies of the lower species. He was a craftsman. An engineer. A fucking artist!

The man was now trying to speak, spurting huge gouts of blood across his face and chest. Pickman extended his two-foot long tubular tongue and licked at it, smacking his lips. From the policeman's ruined abdomen, now spilled treasures, treats, sweetmeats and yummy morsels, scented with the Parmesan tang from the gastric follicles. Somebody screamed – high pitched in F sharp – a man's scream. Then everyone joined in and he heard the sounds of running.

Like a fucking weasel he was on his feet, sprinting between the jostling bodies whose stink offended him so badly. He didn't need to look back to know the hunter was hot on his tail. He started leaping to make speed, knocking pedestrians down like ten-pins, ran straight across a stream of traffic towards the lurid neon-glow of a club entrance. 'The Strange High House In The Mist' – inside would be womb-dark, hot and crowded. More chance of shaking off his pursuer.

Pickman hadn't reckoned on the security. As he crossed the threshold, two bored looking monsters pounced on him. One of them, a colossal black in Tarrantino-chic mirror shades, grabbed his collar. Gills fluttered as the man talked in a thick Telford accent.

"Sorry mate. You're not coming in here."

"Yeah – no fucking jeans allowed," sniggered the equally large skinhead, nodding at Pickman's blood-stained clothes. Short purple fur covered the man's face and naked body.

"Looks like you've been scrapping already mate. Well not in here you fucking don't. It may be the end of civilisation as we know it, but we still don't allow yobboes in our club, you do understand?"

Pickman tore the fucker's windpipe out in one swipe. The man fell back against the wall in a welter of blood, his eyes – all whites – darting around in panic. The black guy let hold of him and backed off.

"Ok, mate, ok. You go in. I don't want any trouble… I get off in half an hour."

Clinical, Brutal....

Pickman slithered past and barrelled down a flight of stairs straight into a wall of rhythmic noise. Deep gut-churning beats collided apocalyptically with grinding metal and electronic shrieking – necrotechno! The latest hit tune from 'Mastectomy.' He knew instantly he'd made a mistake. The noise and the crowding confused him. Heads turned their bored gaze on him. Somewhere in the middle of a heaving mass of bodies, tentacles flailed the air in time with the music. Among the freaks in here he didn't seem too out of place. Then someone shouted his name and he lost all control.

He started lashing out, screaming – people joining him as his claws and teeth rent flesh and sent geysers of blood in all directions. A burly man wearing only a leather rapist mask shrieked as Pickman ripped his arm from the shoulder and swung it round his head like a club, cracking tattooed skulls and spilling drug-fried brains onto the squelchy carpet. Another bouncer shoved his way through the heaving mass and ill-advisedly grappled with him, trying to head-butt him. Pickman caught the man's head between his hands and drove his thumbs straight into his victim's eye-sockets deep into the cranium and brain. The man fell back twitching to the blood soaked floor.

Suddenly Pickman was alone in an empty space – like an arena before the commencement of butchery. People were crawling over each other like chickens trying to reach the exit. He swivelled around looking for cover and stopped. The Assassin stood about twenty yards from him. "Blaze away!" said the man in a dry nasal voice that sounded incredibly bored. Pickman pushed a body away from him, trailing innards. It hit the ground with a wet splat.

"What do you want?" croaked Pickman.

"There's scarcely a man of the crew I haven't had in my barber's chair. Brownbeards, blackbeards, redbeards... I've polished them all off!"

Sirens. Pickman's gaze fell to the Colt Python fondled fetishistically in The Assassin's hand, dangling casually, like a limp cock – not even pointed at him. The man was goading him – inviting him to make a break for it. Fucking Dirty Harry! The Assassin's eyes were black and scorpionic.

"Slashing throats or snapping spines, Tod weltered in his glorious gore, leering and chuckling, winking and nudging his audience to laugh along with him on the road to Hell!"

"Why me?"

Pickman could feel his skin changing in response – felt the ancient, pre-adamite hormones pumping through his bloodstream. Soon small poisonous spines would erupt, blossom into indescribable armour, and he'd be faced with a choice – he could take his chance and try to rip out the bastard's throat, or sit passively and die like a dog. The Assassin smiled innocently. His hair was long and dark, his cheekbones high. Even though he acted casual, his movements and reflexes nevertheless suggested power and speed. This was his business and he was a consummate professional.

"Don't fuck me about now Dicky, I want to watch 'Father Ted' tonight and it's on in half an hour."

"Psychedelics are almost irrelevant in a town where you can wander into a casino any time of the day or night and witness the crucifixion of a gorilla..."

"Don't be cute Dicky, a little birdy tells me you're working for Rex Mundy. And Mundy smells to me like the cheese picked from between the toes of a Himalayan sherpa who hasn't had a bath or changed his socks since England won the fucking World Cup. And the last entry in Fenton's diary says he was going to visit Mr M, who is currently 'away on business'. I want to know where Claudia is."

"Real happiness, in politics, is a wide-open hammer shot on some poor bastard who knows he's been trapped, but can't flee," blathered Pickman, pointing to the dead bodies, "In your culture, popularity may be achieved by bizarre beings and in strange ways."

The Assassin looked bored, but didn't take his eyes off Pickman. There was a crashing noise and some men rushed in from the office beyond the bar. One of them, wearing a Tony Blair mask and a pink tutu, held a sawn-off shotgun that he pointed at The Assassin.

"Right. Put the fucking gun down mate. Then both of you lie down on the floor until the police arrive."

The Assassin didn't even answer. His gun swung up in a blinding arc and fired once. The man's right arm came off at the elbow and smacked wetly into the wall behind him. The man screamed and fell to his knees. The Assassin sniggered. Pickman took his chance and leaped, angelfish spines erupting spectacularly from his body surface, poison-carrying chelicerae sprouting either side of his jaws, which split open three ways, like a rattlesnake's. He really thought he had the bastard where he wanted, but The Assassin twisted unbelievably – like smoke – like a modern-day Mervyn Davies – the gun spat – once – and Pickman saw the world turn Humpty Dumpty, a hole the size of King Kong's tackle gaping in his chest. He felt around it with fingers rapidly going numb – tried to sit up – looked down at the ruin of his abdomen – at his blood, an ocean of it – and pieces of offal – and he tried to scream and tasted his own vomit filling his mouth.

The hunter stood above him.

"Come on now Pickman, where's my poisonous sweetheart?"

Pickman spat and kicked out with one venomous spurred hoof – only one was responding. The hunter sidestepped frowning, shrugged and fired again into Pickman's groin.

"Tell me now and maybe I'll be nice and kill you quickly."

"EVERYTHING IS BETTER IN THE ASS. Cocaine, wine, coffee, nitrous (supposedly quite dangerous), sushi, "Little Mermaid" DVDs, cat food, Forth: EVERYTHING is better if you put it in your ass. Everything!"

Pickman shook like a rat in a terrier's jaws. Blood and vomit and cold sweat spattered the hunter's coat. His eyes cleared suddenly and he gazed at The Assassin in wonder.

"You are the angel of death."

A siren – close, voices, footsteps... the hunter smiled at Pickman.

"Close enough." He said, pointed the gun into his face... a roaring noise and blinding white light...

Clinical, Brutal....

Whitechapel

Radcliff Gregory

I'd seen his eyes,
dark and sharp like struck flint
between the cobblestones and stars.
From a distance,
they hid beneath his hat brim,
waiting spark out of their eclipse.

Through Whitechapel,
I stalked him, my eyes matched his,
growing darker by each passing midnight.
His shadow gorged
on grimy lamplight, expanding
round each hibernating corner.

I'd seen his eyes,
moments before their intimacy with mine;
moments after their intimacy with mine.
His Saville Row suit
tail slipped through my fingers,
gentlemanly in its caress.

Its silk thrilled me,
hardened a blood-rush
against my own Cheapside cloth.

Following him,

thinking the backward glance meant something,

watching as he paused to piss

in my eyeline,

smiling, he was watching me watching him;

smiling, as he shook it dry and stroked it hard;

then walked onwards,

nearly decent, his black case snapped shut.

He walked with slow purpose.

I paused to spend,

then readied myself, hard enough

for his professional eyes.

I trod his piss

reverently, savouring his juice,

and walked on, rubbing just enough

and I saw him,

his eyes, wild as his prick,

intimate with mine; his breathing

came thick and fast

with mine, sticky on my skin,

where it colluded with whore blood.

Clinical, Brutal....

Slab

Jock Drummond

It was a fucking mess alright. I've been in this job for years and I've seen some pretty fucking gruesome sights. But this cunt took the fucking biscuit. Rab was out back, spewing his fucking guts up. Ordinarily I'd've called him a fucking pussy, but this time I was willing to make an exception. It was all I could do to keep myself from giving the boak too.

'What d'ye want us to do, chief?' a wee prick uniform asked unsteadily, a look of anguish on his pallid face.

I looked him up and down and felt sorry for the cunt.

'Youse new on the job?' I asked. I'd not seen him about before.

'Not really, just new to this area,' he said, 'but I've never seen anything like this.'

'I don't think any of us have,' I consoled. I have to admit that I was in shock. I mean, I'm pretty hardened to all of this shite, but sometimes you see something that really strikes you to your core, truly horrifies you.

'I've never smelled anything like this either,' piped up Ronnie, the first CSI to arrive on the scene, as he crossed the threshold. 'You're lookin' a bit peely wally, our Jimmy,' he said, clocking the uniform.

'No shit,' Jimmy quailed.

'Actually....' another uniform, Bob Roberston, a good fella who I've known for years, piped up.

'Actually, what Bob?' I asked even though I wasn't entirely sure I wanted to know.

'There is shit, chief. Lots of it. Jobbie fuckin' everywhere in the next room.'

'Right.' This is getting nastier by the minute. 'Any idea who the shite belongs tae?'

'Nope,' Bob says, shaking his head. 'I was hoping forensics could help us with that. But you have to see it.'

'Really? Do I absolutely fucking have to? Or are ye just being a cunt and trying to make my really bad day even fucking worse?'

'No chief, not at all. But really, you have to see it to fuckin' believe it. It's... it's... it's like nothing I've seen. It's fuckin' horrific.'

I nod and turn to Ronnie. 'Ronnie, what're the chances you could get your guys onto the shite through here?' Ronnie hesitates and makes to speak. 'Follow me and Bob,' I gesticulate and head after Bob, with Ronnie reluctantly trailing behind.

Holy fuck! We're in the main living room. It looks fucking disgusting and smells even fucking worse. 'It's shite alright,' I say. We're practically up to our oxters in it.

'Fuckin' hell!' Ronnie gags and makes a sharp u-turn.

Me, I'm made of sterner stuff but this is seriously testing me to my physical limits here. 'Ok, I've seen enough,' I tell Bob and turn to follow Ronnie. I can tell Bob's not far behind me.

'Youse!' a crabbit auld cunt shouts as she emerges from her flat a floor above, up on the third.

I look up. 'Me?'

'Aye, polis?'

'Aye,' I concede.

'Hoo lang's this gunnae g'wan fir?' she batters, a scowl on her surly grey features.

'I'm afraid I don't know, madam,' I confess. 'Has anyone been up to see you get?'

'What?' the deaf old bat bawls at me.

'I said, has anyone been up to see you yet?'

'Aye. They told me they'd be back later to ask me some questions and that I should stay put the noo.'

'Then we'd very much appreciate it if you would,' I retort. Interfering old bag.

We all go outside to get some air as the forensics guys begin to arrive in full force. The premises is now fully cordoned off, too, although the trouble with these tenements is that you have to seal off the back exit and the lane as well, and also the close which makes access for the other residents pretty much impossible while you've got forensics combing the scene. And being communal areas, the lanes are pains in the arse to search for evidence at the best of times. So here we are, standing in the back lane of a very standard tenement in Partick on a Thursday night in the middle of fucking November. It's been dreich as fuck all day and the rain's starting to get heavier.

Ronnie's still heaving and retching and I think he's got a chunk of carrot or something in his thrapple because he's coughing and spluttering like an old banger. I give him a sharp thump between the shoulder blades and that seems to shift it.

'Tha's pure fuckin' boggin' in there,' he manages to gasp when he's recovered his breath.

'Aye, that it is, that it is,' I concur and I must admit I'm still dazed and could use a couple of bevvies.

'So d'ye henk it was some chancer who fucked up bigstyle, or...?' Jimmy quavered, speaking for the first time in a while. He's still got flecks of spew in the corners of his mouth and is as white as a fucking sheet, the poor cunt.

'Ach, I fucking doubt it,' I opine. 'The only thing I can be sure of on the strength of what I've seen so far is that this is the work of one – or more – sick fucking bawbag cunts.'

'Hey, chief!' a voice comes from the doorway out to the back that we've come out of. Sounds like Inspector Millar, known ironically as Grinner on account of his being a stern-faced mealy-mouthed cunt. 'Are youse comin' back in here?'

'Aye,' I call back. 'I'd rather no', but if I must... I'm gettin' drookit out here anyway.'

'Aye,' he hollers back. 'Ah henk ye should see this...'

***

It's late when I get to knock off for the night. The forensics guys will be there for a fucking long time yet, but there's precious little I can do at least until morning so I tag along with Bob for a couple of half and halfs in the Lismore. It's not a million miles from home for me and is also the closest place to the hellhole we've just left, both being on Dumbarton Road. It's also a bit more upmarket than the Three Judges which does ok beer if you like that sort of thing but is a bit loud and a bit spit an' sawdust for my tastes. The Lismore has a few decent malts on – and I'm partial to a dram of Highland malt – and is a better place for a chat. Poor Bob's still as white as a sheet, the poor cunt.

'I hadn't been expecting that second body either,' I confess in a low tone. 'Here, get these down ye. Ye look like you need it even more than I do. And I fucking need it, believe me!'

He sank the half pint of Deuchar's in a single gulp, and followed it with the double twelve year-old Old Pulteney. I followed suite and ordered again. The woman handed me my change and this time we made it as far as a table before starting on our drinks.

'Fuck,' Bob muttered under his breath, staring into his beer.

'I know,' I say, shaking my head.

'Fuck. I cannae mind having seen anything like that,' he trembles.

'Same here,' I concur.

'Fuck. I mean... that was seriously fucked up shit in there.'

'Aye. With the emphasis on the shit,' I say, trying to lighten the mood, but feeling as stunned as I knew Bob was.

We sat for a while in silence, staring at the table top, sticky with rings from the bottoms of pint glasses, working through our own thoughts. Reliving the horrors we had seen in the last few hours. Knowing we'd never be able to erase those images, no matter how hard we tried. Knowing we'd witnessed something we could never escape from. Knowing we had touched something, been to a place from which we could never return.

'I don't envy ye,' Bob said at last.

'I don't fucking envy me either,' I said wearily.

Just before we'd knocked off our shifts, the Super had rung me and broken the news that I'd be heading this case. Fuck. I'd never seen Smiler look so fucking happy in his miserable fucking life. I've never been entirely sure what that cunt's got against me, but he's always been pretty clear that he likes to see me suffer. Maybe it's nothing personal and I'm just being paranoid. Some people are born sadistic cunts, after all.

'Same again?' asked Bob, rising from his stool.

'Aye,' I nodded. I knew I had to be up in the morning and I knew I had to face all this fucking shite all over again and in the cold light of day, but for now... Fuck it, I was gonna get blethered.

***

Morning came too fucking soon. I'd put a few away, but hadn't succeeded in remotely erasing the memories of what I'd seen the day before. My constitution being what it is, I wasn't suffering from any symptoms of a hangover, although I wasn't sure how well my stomach would hold if presented with similar scenes today. Credit where it's due, the boys on the night shift had done a pretty fucking good job of trawling through all the shite – literal and metaphorical – of gathering information and getting the scene cleaned up. At least it meant that the remaining residents of the tenement could get on with their everyday lives, or as much as that's possible with the press camped outside and knowing that a double murder took place in the house just the day before. Still, such things are outwith my control, even if I am in charge of the investigation.

I've got uniforms doing the door-to-door stuff right now. I'll pay anyone a visit that looks like they might be of interest, but right now I've another problem. I'm down at the morgue having a pow-wow and chewing the fat with the head coroner. He looks pretty fucking harassed. I must admit that I've been harassing him pretty hard myself since I clocked on. I need answers and I need them fast, like fucking yesterday.

'I've been working on these for a while the now,' he's telling me. 'Progress has been slower than usual, because, well, frankly, these poor cunts are a fucking mess.'

'Tell me about it,' I sigh.

And here's the fucking problem. Sure, I have to find out which sick fuck or fucks are responsible, and hunt the fuckers down, then piece a case together that'll bring the cunts to justice. Yes, when I catch these sick pricks there'll be hell to pay and then some. They'll wish they'd never been fucking born. Of course, I'll have to establish motive, hope that forensics can piece together enough evidence to prove that they were there and all that shite. But before I can start on any of that, I have to figure out who the poor cunts down here under the cold white lights of the morgue are exactly. We need to ID the carved up, ruined cunts on the slab, and it's not going to be easy. Partly because the flat was supposed to be vacant. And partly – mostly – because of the fucking state they're in.

'We're still working on cause of death for the male,' Stevie, the coroner is telling me, 'although we think we have a pretty good idea. We just need to investigate further to confirm my opinion.'

The male was the first body we'd found. The cliché of a victim having a face like a hamburger wasn't appropriate here. Too much of an understatement. His head was fucking pulp.

'Go on.'

'Well, white, average height and build, aged approximately 35. Cause of death is still 50/50,' Stevie grimaces. 'Exanguination is one option. Blunt forced trauma is the other. It depends if they stoved his cranium in before or after they disembowelled him and pulled his intestines out through his abdominal wall.'

'What the fuck?'

'I know, it's pretty fucked up. I mean, I've seen some pretty brutal stuff in my time, but this fucking takes the cake. We're still trying to deduce precisely what was used to slit the belly in such a way. Looks like he was pretty much cut from the pelvis in an upward, sawing motion with a sharp knife – a kitchen knife or somesuch, with a long, straight, unserrated blade – till the attacker hit the sternum. The entrails – specifically the lower intestine, the colon – had been cut, an incision several inches long, and the contents... *removed*.'

'...and smeared all over the walls...' I finished.

'So I've heard.'

'What about the blunt forced trauma?'

'Ah, yes. As you can probably tell just from looking, a large number of blows – probably in the region of forty or even fifty, suggesting a sustained attack that was more than a mere frenzy – to the skull, both front and back, which would have caused massive haemorrhaging and a very swift death, albeit still a very fucking painful one. He would have only felt the first two or three blows, I would imagine.'

I'm trying hard not to imagine. The victim's nose and eyeballs are buried somewhere in the snot-like pulp that constituted the remainder of his brain. His bottom jaw is hanging off, smashed to smithereens. His upper jaw is barely there, and what there is of it contains only a few splinters of tooth. This is bad. Really fucking bad.

'As you can see, he was knocked about a bit, too, perimortem. His torso is a mass of extremely severe contusions...'

Indeed it is. His pale skin, through which the massive gash that runs from his pubic area to the middle of his ribcage is riven with ultra-livid bruises of all hues.

'There's one other thing,' Bob adds, raising his finger, a perplexed look on his graggy features.

'Aye?'

'His rectum had been cut out.'

'What the fuck?' I'm aghast.

'I know. See here?' he asks, turning the corpse on its side for me to see. His arsehole is enormous, a huge crater, large enough for me to insert my fist should I have been perverse enough to want to, surrounded by dried blood.

'What... did forensics find it?' It seemed absurd even then, to be asking if our guys had managed to find a missing arsehole. Under any other circumstances, I'd've probably laughed my own arse off.

'In all that mess? Actually, as a matter of fact they did. His sphincter...' Bob splutters slightly. 'His sphincter had been placed over where his mouth was.'

'Are you shitting me?' I ask, agog.

'I shit ye not,' he sighs. 'These are seriously fucked up wee pricks you're looking for.'

'And the second body...?' I hardly dare ask. I know I need to know, but really don't want to know the grisly details.

'Female,' Stevie confirms. I hadn't been entirely sure when I'd seen the bloody mess that had been spread about that shite-strewn living room the night before, although I'd had my suspicions based on the shreds of clothing that had been left in tatters on the floor. 'Late twenties, I'd say.'

'How far have you got with her?'

'Well, again, not as far as I'd have hoped, and certainly not as far as her killer or killers... but really... she's in a serious fucking way. I'm not sure if I've ever seen a body this badly fucking mangled. I mean, sure, car accidents, fires, three months in a river, you expect it to be pretty fucking nasty. Putrefaction's one thing, but this was clearly a single sustained attack and she's fucking mincemeat.'

'So what've youse got so far? Cause of death? Details of the attack?'

'Also disembowelled. Her lower intestine and bowel had actually been extracted through her vagina via an enforced prolapse. Initial investigations suggest that a large object was inserted manually and with some force and used in order to achieve partial excision... otherwise, the injuries are largely consistent with those sustained by the male...' Nevertheless, he continued to list them all, in the minutest medial detail, and talked on in this way for quite some time.

After a while, his words ceased to register. The whole deal was fucked up and foul, and it pained me to know that when – not if, but when – we caught the psycho cunts responsible, there was no penalty the law could put their way that could come even remotely close to serving justice.

But first things first. We had to figure out who the hell these people were lying here. Once we'd done that, we'd need to locate their next of kin and call them in. I felt bad for them. Bob and his team were extremely skilled, but nothing in the world was going to make these two pieces of meat look even vaguely presentable.

Clinical, Brutal....

Last Seen Wearing

Lucius Rofocale

Alice Benjamin went missing between 21st - 23rd June, 2009.

She is 21, 5'3, brunette, slim with shoulder length hair. Her eyes are brown.

Alice was wearing blue jeans and a black top cut off at the arms. She usually walks listening to music on her ipod.

Have you seen her?

What Have I Done To Your Daughter?

Lucius Rofocale

I am the man your parents warned you about
I will fuck you then leave
because I am empty

I have nothing else to offer.

Clinical, Brutal....

ACTION // CUT

Stuart Bateman

CUT /////// SPLICE ///////
CUT /////// SLICE ///////
CUT /////// SPLICE ///////
CUT /////// SLICE ///////
CARVE /// SPLICE ///
CARVE /// DICE ///
CARVE /// DICE ///
CARVE /// DICE ///
CARVE /// DICE ///
CARVE /// DICE ///

SPAMONRYE (Sounds of Sadism)

Karl van Cleave

I didn't recognize her for a CSV importer though
While Internet needs major repairs
Notes and organizes
Anti spoofing Anti Spam Lotus Notes
Integration integrates with both feet
Superficially, they play it.

But I could hear
Through the walls
The sounds
Of Sadism

20,000 leagues
and an internet collective
turds stored in the cupboard

Small wonder she looked rough leaving the house for work some
mornings.

Business Forms Bookfunction as an election year that protects and
forces email programs
There are bound by it, although this type of AntiSpam Tool Kit: Paul
Wolfe, Charlie Scott, Mike Erwin: Books. Web Antispam Wired anti
spam and Eudora Mail.

Clinical, Brutal....

Tags: Viruses, Virus, trojan, western union. They have installed SPAM PROTECTION.

Publicity Hound 3434 County Sentinel
You have dominated recent headlines did more than show how badly the site of all, you.
As long as a text message from Nelson, BC, Canada writes: Oooh, now the book I would like it out there.

He's going to hunt you down.

You know it.

Room

Karl van Cleave

Take a look around
This room

Do it
         Do it with fresh eyes
Do it with peeled eyes
Stripping
The skin
Of your eyelids
Back

You'll never leave
You cannot leave
Taste the blade
Tongue out now

Taste   Taste   Taste

Now touch

Touch it
Touch it

Clinical, Brutal....

How does it

        Feel?

Touch   Touch   Touch

Inhale deeply

Do it

Do as you're told

Sensory overload

Soon you won't even remember

Feel the burn

How does it

           Feel?

Soon you won't even remember what sense is

       So just take it

          And love it

             You hear that, do you?

               Well, *do* you?

The roar of the big machine

Throbbing

Growing

Pulsating

Sit with me a while

       Talk

Let's talk philosophy

While you still have a tongue in your head

Reproach – dreadful blasphemies – a finger twister, frigging violently,
the stench of blood rising, swallow hard
An impending amputation

Spread, bound
Making no sound
Embuggered
Silent and still
How does it

                          Feel?

Tell me
In detail

                Tell me

Can you   feel?

Feel the heat, the burn, the torment
A tension building
Steps forward,
Poised
        Machine aflame
        Engorged
First utterance
Inchoate

Clinical, Brutal....

Red mist

Venom in his eyes

      weakly

            discharges

Surgery

Vincent Clasper

Dr Belton, The Revolution Star, had built up quite a following and widespread reputation during the three years he had been practising his trade. Qualifying had taken him eight whole years and had been a struggle: he'd almost had a breakdown prior to his graduation. Belton and stress were a poor combination, unhappy bedfellows. Pressure always had an adverse effect upon his health. Bouts of 'flu, fever, exhaustion, fainting and German Measles were frequent.

"This Heaven gives me migraine," he often complained, closing down the surgery for a week or so each month as he took to his sickbed in convalescence. Clients always proved keen for his rapid recovery as they clamoured urgently for a dose of his Godlike advice. His very words and presence could cure many aliments, from the common cold, to love, to AIDS. His world renown had brought him fame and fortune. He had been the progenitor of The Revolution. He was their Star. His life was complete, full to the brim with his work, his head constantly buzzed with ideas for radical new cures and remedies for the most obscure and otherwise incurable complaints and conditions.

He sat nervously in his brilliant white surgery surroundings, the DIY furniture about him surgically cleansed, the low-emission PC monitor displaying unfathomable new theories and formulas, which he fed out to his myriad legion of disciples world-wide. The following gained by the Dr Belton School of Revolutionary Autosurgery was wholly phenomenal in its extent. The respectable DesTech Medical

Engineering Co. calendar upon the sterilely clean white wall behind him showed the year to be February, 2004. Nostradamus had been proven wrong, by the hand of Belton. He crossed his legs, glanced down at the brown Brogue suspended from the base of his spindly leg, carefully tidied his papers and finally pressed the intercom button and spoke to his secretary:

"Er, okay, s-send in whoever's next…er, Mr Dryer, I think."

"Certainly," the voice returned, the voice of Della Montegran, the Cleavage Queen, Belton's long-time lover and asexual partner.

The latch clicked as Mr Dryer entered the arena. His face wrinkled slightly as the deathly clean scent met his nostrils. The smell was sharp in pitch, as though the whole surgery had died and been embalmed in order to preserve it for eternal posterity, an eternal testament to the greatness of The Revolution Star. He surveyed to room and stood, manfully hiding his apprehension before stepping toward the desk.

"Take a seat," said The Revolution Star, turning on his swivel chair. Nothing had been expensive in here. The chair had cost a mere £15. Consultation sessions with Dr Belton were considerably less cheap. A month's decent wages for an hour was not an unremarkable fee considering the Doctor's reputation. The cost of a cure for many of Belton's clients was, however, sanity.

Daniel Dryer sat stroking the knife in his pocket whilst looking directly at the Doctor's pallid, blemished face, his eyes watery behind the dense convex of his spectacles. Belton's look merely glanced flickeringly at Dryer, whose hard, sharp eyes, slightly glazed by mania, unnerved him. That Dryer did indeed have a rather piercing look is true, but then Belton rarely looked directly at his clients. They all unnerved him rather. Dan took a vending machine packet of Marlboro and a box of Bass Taverns matches from the pocket of his red and green plaid shirt, the design of which he was certain belied his true coolness. A wolf in sheep's clothing, an angel in Devil's boots, he would bide his time until it was right. He would know.

The Cleavage Queen entered, clad in tight white denim jeans, high-lacing black patent leather stiletto-heeled boots and a semi-opaque white blouse, through which one could discern a revealing fleshtone bra. Her pointing nipples thrust against the flimsy fabric, while her waist length dark brown hair swayed gently in time to an inverse rhythm set by her distinct hip movement. Slinky. She placed a tray bearing a large pitcher of water and two glasses upon the table. Belton couldn't take tea, coffee or chocolate, as all three induced serious migraines. His clients, too, were only offered water. Chilled, but not iced. It was economical, environmentally and politically sound, and prevented them from developing caffeine-induced agitation whilst in the surgery. Dan studied the Cleavage Queen as she lasciviously slid past him, her pert buttocks almost touching his arm as she bent to place the tray, he barely disguising his naked lust. His left eyebrow was raised as the insides of his cheeks began to run with saliva, his blood circulating in futile arousal. He lit a cigarette and drew on it, hard, his burning eyes tracking her feminine form as she slunk past him and back toward the door, the scent of hormones, musk and ozone streaking the atmosphere back to his flaring nostrils in her wake.

"Excuse me," Belton attempted to interject feebly.

Dan's mind was no longer in the surgery, but in the library, dimly lit and softly focused. The images seeped forth and trickled through the quiet, narrow aisles between the shelves as Della slowly unfastened the thin blouse…

'Touch me…watch me…' she whispered hypnotically as she began to unbutton her jeans.

Trance-like, he raised his hands toward her heaving breasts and ran his tongue around his lips as the sweat trickled to reach her collar…she moaned seductively as she drew her jeans to her knees…

"So, er, what seems to be the problem, Mr er…" Belton referred to his notes briefly before looking back at the diminutive fellow across the desk. "…Dryer? And can you please put that out?"

Jolted sharply back to the harsh surroundings of the surgery, Dan blinked, coughed slightly, sucked again on the cigarette, exhaled casually, reclined confidently in the moulded plastic chair and began:

"I'm suffering from this terrible insomnia… I can't seem to escape my thoughts, you know? It's affecting me really badly… the thing is, I can't decide if I'm at fault or not, you know, or if they are… Sometimes I feel so dried up, so empty, so, like, devoid of interesting conversation, and I just can't communicate with them. What do I say to them, I mean, what is there? …I can't go for all that trivial, tedious small talk; it's so *boring* and pointless. There are times when I just can't be bothered with them, their shallowness, their stupidity. But y'know, deep down when I really think about it, I know that I'm right, you know? They just don't understand, because they don't think… but it still grieves me. It really stresses me out, it keeps me awake at night…"

The Revolution Star sat and listened patiently, nodding. He arched an eyebrow above the metal frames upon his sallow featured face in a somewhat hostile manner, hiding his mouth behind his fingers as he rested his chin. Beneath the table, the legs were crossed and the buttocks clenched. He glanced at the computer monitor, linked to the most advanced, state-of-the-art unit on the market, then back to his client.

"They just don't get it, you see," Dryer continued. "The world's all wrong. Democracy's such a bad system, because they're all fools. They can't think for themselves!" Growing excited, Dryer again raised his dense eyebrow as if a cynical look of feigned surprise would give suitable emphasis to his claim. "The world needs a benevolent dictator. And I'm the man for the job. See, I was reading Nietzsche, and…"

Belton inhaled boredly before proclaiming his diagnosis. He could fix this imbecile. As the man at the fore of radical remedies, Belton had heard of the so-called Thought Virus, and rejected it as outmoded in theoretical terms, unprovable in practice, inaccurate as a prognosis, and, in short, utter piffle. Like RSI and ME, TV was an hypochondriac's complaint, a stupid fabrication.

"You're studying right now, I believe," he pronounced presumptuously.

Dryer nodded.

"I think that that's your problem. You're not *applying* yourself fully. You need a job, to fill your head and occupy your time properly, constructively. Get into the work routine, you won't have *time* to *think* about petty angsts… the Real World of Work will make you use your head properly, rather than filling it with this pointless academic drivel, which is completely useless, you don't need it anyway. You'll learn to socialise better and become more tolerant. University's a rather poor agent, socially, you know… and, you see, once you get busy and forget these feeble concerns, you'll find you're much more content and realise how insignificant your worries are. It's not the real world, you see… And you'll be so tired after a real nine to five shift, you won't need to go out, so you won't meet people who'll annoy you. You'll sleep well, appreciate weekends and bank holidays, so you can go DIY shopping and driving, give up drink, lose interest in sex, forget music, television and stuff, you won't have *time*... decorate the house, vote Tory...

"Okay? Come on, give up the education, it's not healthy, it promotes independent thought, it's counterproductive to the system, it's a waste of taxpayers' money... students don't put anything back in, you know, it's *my* tax money they live on. Get a job. And get out, I've got people waiting..."

***

Next up, Huw Collins, who slithered in, leaving a silver train in his carefully contrived wake. The dazzling lighting, reflected and intensified by the brilliant, clinical white walls and ceiling, caused the oil in his painstakingly arranged quiff to shimmer and shine, almost taking on an affected half-life of its own. Slippery, moist, Collins slewed and swaggered across the tiles and slid into the chair across the bespoke desk from the consultant, whose complexion was growing paler by the quarter hour, waxier by the moment, and his eyes more glazed by the second. Legs crossed, fists clenched, The Revolution Star turned on his carefully selected revolving chair, a suave, officious black and grey affair set upon five castors.

"So...", he wheezed, eyes popping slightly, "er....uh, Mr Col... um, Collins?"

"Yep, 's me," replied Huw, oozing sickly-sweet smelling confidence, quiff slowly melting in the heat of the interrogatively poised desk lamp.

The Cleavage Queen spilled in through the door, her bosoms resting on the white plastic tray that bore the customary jug and two glasses. She flicked her hair and passed a blatantly indifferent glance in Collins' direction. Her metal-tipped stilettos clattered evenly against the meticulously scrubbed floor tiles, her blouse pulled taught across her firm and proportionally ample breasts. She looked with boredom toward Belton as she placed the drinks on the desk, tossed her hair once more as she turned, and sleekly departed, just as she had entered. Della really was a fox. A fantasy, and no doubt.

"Er...what seems to be the, uh, problem, um...nnnnnggggh... Mr, uh, Collinsss?" strained the doctor.

"Well," the brash youth opposite The Revolution Star began, "I've 'ad a string o' birds, right, they've all left me, me dad's died recently, I've got no friends, I'm bored o' clubbin,' yeh, an' I'm just downright depressed. Me life's shit, right. Everybody hates me, an' I just don't know what to do. I got no aims, no, 'obbies, nothin'...I..."

"One...moment..." interjected Dr Belton. "I see...uh." He breathed carefully once more. "You seem to be...er, suffering from...a...acute boredom...caused by a lack of direction and application, you know...er...ah...no routine, or...anything." A rather pained look crossed Belton's face for a fleeting moment, before his lungs deflated and his fingers relaxed once more to a normal grip upon his pen. "What you need is a job...to give you something real, to fill yourself with something worthwhile, rather than these idle worries, petty teenage anxieties...once you're employed, you'll realise how insignificant all this is, okay?"

Clinical, Brutal....

Collins looked perturbed, and opened his mouth, preparing to speak, to voice his incredulity, but Belton continued impassively prior to his reorientation.

"...If you could sign the...urrr, necessary documents at, er, reception on the, ah, way out... my um, secretary will... ah, deal... with you... and give my regards to your father..."

Still shaken, Collins rose from the chair and headed for the door. His quiff remained immaculate, but his oozing confidence has seeped from him almost instantaneously. He was pale and clearly rattled by the Doctor's almost inhuman lack of heartlessness and lack of consideration or sympathy.

Once again alone in his surgery, Belton gasped and glanced at his watch, his bowels abrim and demanding permission to relax. The Doctor, meanwhile had no time nor wish to take time out to relieve himself. Not away from home, and certainly not while others were in the building, Della in particular. Such things are so...embarrassing...bodily functions are not the kind of thing one ever admitted to ever occurring. They're unclean, unnatural, and, well, disgusting. Quite frankly, they're wholly unmentionable. So he had to hold out for the close of surgery. It shouldn't prove exceptionally difficult, with only one client remaining to be seen during today's session.

He pressed the intercom button on his desk and spoke to his secretary. "Er...D...uh, bring me something to chew on, could you, ah, please..." he gasped as the pressure in his lower abdomen reached an almost intolerable level.

Ms Montegran sloped in, casually seductive with her usual air of disaffection and handed him an apple, organically grown. No biscuits: far too unhealthy. Chocolate was out, because it induced the worst migraines of all, and gum…well, most gum was mint-flavoured, and the taste of mint appalled and offended the Doctor's sensitive palette.

Teeth gritted, nails scratching into the surface of his desk, Belton gasped in a pained tone for her to send in the final client of the day. The Cleavage Queen nodded, a wry smirk flitting across her small, tight-pinched mouth as she left. Moments later a short, rounded young woman in her early twenties entered. Her straight hair was cut into a jaw-length bob with a fringe, giving her an appearance that seemed inappropriate for her years. Her eyes, like her hair, were dark brown, and in keeping with her excessive attempt to appear younger, she was attired in clothes more suited to a fourteen year old, and a tarty one at that. Her blue denim shirt was unfastened so as to expose considerable amounts of cleavage, and her legs, to which bright red tights clung, were exposed from the mid-thigh, the point at which her blue denim a-line skirt ended.

"Hiya," she chirped through her slightly crooked and curiously-held teeth, "I'm Lena Bee, and I think you can help me… you see, I've got several problems, and there doesn't seem to be anyone who really understands, and there's absolutely no-one who's at all willing to try and help me. You see, first of all, I went to a party last weekend, and there was this boy and he already had a girlfriend, but we both got really drunk and his girlfriend wasn't there and we ended up getting off a bit and now we've started to see each other but she doesn't know about me and I feel such a bitch and I know it's unfair and… Well, the thing is, I really like him and I know he really likes me and wants to sleep with me and I want to sleep with him to, but I can't, because…

"Well, the problem is, I'm Christian and I don't really believe in sex before marriage, and I wonder what it'd be like to marry him, he's such a sweetie…" She drew breath and continued. "I became Christian a few days before my sixteenth birthday, just when I was thinking 'great, I can get laid now', and I was at a sleepover with some friends and we'd gone to sleep and something woke me up and I saw light through the window and then I saw the sheet move and I realised that there must be a God, and one of my friends saw it too so I wasn't dreaming, I swear, and from then on we were both Christians, and it's the best thing that's ever happened to us, and I've met lots of gorgeous, sweet chaps through the church, and it's a bit of a bugger 'cause I can't sleep with any of them unless I get married.

"Can you get to the point?" The Revolution Star demanded. "How…" he paused and gasped for breath, a pain gripping him from within. "How exactly can I *help* you?"

His patient looked shocked. "Oh. Yes. Well, anyway, there are some other guys I know, and I think that they're real darlings but they don't like one of my other friends who's really cute, they're really mean to him and say that they only do it because he's nasty to them, but I don't think it's fair of them and I don't know what to do because I like them all, and they're lovely people and I get these feelings and oh, and it upsets me when they don't all get on, I don't like it when my friends don't all get on…"

Belton gasped and wrestled himself into stillness. "I…it…t's…your…f…fantasy, …um, uh, right?"

"I guess you could say that, I mean love is a spiritual thing, but there is a physical side to it, and all of my friends are so lovely and I love them all so much, and I just want them all together…"

"Uuuuhhhhhhh…hh…hold on…", gagged the Doctor from his side of the table. By this point, his eyes were bugging and streaming with tears, every muscle in his body was as tense as a tripwire, and his complexion was predominantly as white as the proverbial moving sheet of God save for the red tinge upon his cheeks, present due to the immense strain he was placing on his system. "Mmmmnnnggh…er, I was…uh, j-j-just nnng…w…won…wonder…ing, uh…"

As he struggled to formulate his sentences and to move his mouth but not his bowels, Belton was becoming increasingly aware of the fact that this Lena Bee was alarmingly similar to a girl he had known many years before whilst in school. Yes, he'd been interested, but too afraid to pursue whatever may have come from their relationship potential. Not wishing to admit this, however, he'd projected his yearning onto his friend, feigning to himself and all others concerned that he valued his friendship with both of them so much that he wanted nothing to spoil the utopian situation of the time. Soon after, she'd seemingly changed for the worse, and had begun sacrificing her nights of worship for wild drunken parties, several of which had seen her embarrass herself intensely, the more memorable instances of which had involved her encountering the boyfriends of other girls and undressing in front of all of the other guests. The only thing that had prevented her from being branded the ultimate common slag was her reluctance to bed any of the men involved. Oh, but she wanted to. A wannabe slag, and no mistake. But her religion had had its benefits, then, it could be argued.

In a successful attempt to erase this part of his life from his memory, The Revolution Star had immersed himself in his schooling. Now, in the real world of work, he'd reached the point whereby he'd even managed to forget the name of the girl he'd known all those years ago. All he could recall at this point was that the girl opposite him bore a striking resemblance to the girl from whenever it may have been, if it had ever happened at all in reality. She did bear a considerable resemblance to a girl he recalled vaguely from dreams. The persistence of memory can be driven into the subconscious and manifest itself variously, although Belton strenuously argued against this theory. Her look was similar, her manner and her approach to life was the same, and for some reason he wanted to shag this silly little tart, there and then, on the couch. All the things about this girl in his surgery at this moment brought reminders of the time before the Revolution, with whoever she may have been before flooding back to the poor Doctor, affecting his balance and urges. Hell, even her breasts had that same low-slung look about them. He wanted to look… it was all a little too much for him.

A dense brown fluid began to run from his ears, mouth and nose, and he began to twitch convulsively. As the spasms became stronger and further out of control, Lena actually stopped talking for the first time since she had entered, and looked at her therapist with concern.

"Oooh, are you alright?" she asked dumbly.

"Ffffffffffine…….." hissed Belton as the matter began to flow with greater force from his orifices.

"Okay," said Lena, and drew breath once more to continue her tale. "The thing is, I can't really decide if I want five or six kids, and I really do want to get laid, but God… well, then there's…"

At this point, the Doctor's condition took a turn for the worse, and his control was truly lost. Phrases with no meaning, disjointed and unnecessary spewed forth from his mouth, along with several litres of excrement. "Get it??" he howled as the faecal matter flew, "Get a fucking job, get real, you cunting hapless bint!! You absolute waste of space pious cunt!!! You just don't get it, you're not in the real world. No

I'm *not* out of touch, I *am* the real world, and I can have lots of fucking sex, if I want… I'm a living legend! And if you are who I think you are, then I never fancied you, it was all a con, I just wanted to corrupt you… and I always thought your tits were too fucking saggy for me, you dopey bitch! I know you want me, but I can have anyone… but I'm generous, and want all my clients to be cured…" Belton bellowed as he began to unfasten his trousers.

"Anyway, I'm an atheist, you slaaaag! And I am omnipotent! So come on over and give it up, right now! Get yer fucking kit off, get on the table and give it to me! Getchyer tits out, now!! I wanna get my lips 'round those sagging wabs o' yours! Yes, the world of work is where it's at, motherfucker!!!!!"

Lena rose from her chair in horror as the foul stench filled the room and shit flew through the air, coating the sharp white walls and her own being from head to toe. Was this a part of the famed Dr Belton's Radical Therapy Technique. If so, then she was genuinely dubious as to its worth and the deservedness of the Doctor's reputation.

By this point, Belton was revolving upon his chair at a phenomenal speed, excrement being hurled in all directions, its source seemingly endless. His head was slowly caving in on itself and his body was withering away as he spun, the ordure seeping and slipping from his every pore and oozing down every object in the room. The walls, desk, chair and telephone were truly caked, while Lena looked as though she had spent the last hour and a half mud-wrestling. The smell and texture of the slimy substance which filled the area made it quite evident that this was not the case.

With an eldritch scream that would remain with the traumatised Lena for the rest of her life, the Revolution Star imploded with a vile sounding and even viler smelling slopping, squelching sound, and was finally still. Upon the excreta-dripping chair lay the shrunken, hollow skin of Belton's haemorrhaged body. The surgery fell silent, save for the dripping sounds of the departed Doctor's shit-laden innards as they dropped from the furniture, walls and ceiling, as well as the hem of the wench's skirt, her hands and her face. Her senses awoke from their entranced state, she screamed and fled from the surgery.

***

The headline in the following morning's paper read 'Revolutionary Doctor Dies.'

"He was full of shit anyway," the coroner said.

Sudan

Constance Stadler

The vulture is patient.
Last stage evisceration
The stumble of thirst
of a death intended life.
No "collateral damage".
You are incidental refuse.
A comma in the litany
of carrion
inhumanity.
A rogue profiteer
arcs renegade machete
assuming your status
by the placement of your
rot.

The vulture approaches
his awaited reward.
O
sweet
toddler eyes.

Originally published in *Counterexample Poetics*.

Clinical, Brutal....

Femicide

Constance Stadler

Henna tattooed
Kohl rimmed
Sun burnished
It was permitted.
　　　　The goat hide slid.
　　　　　　Whisking in
　　　　　　fluent chador
　　　　　　　　　so
　　　　　　impeccably cloaked
　　　　　　For the black place.

In fresh slaughter stench
and swelling ululations
　　　I tasted blood intensity
　　　　　　hovering at the cusp
　　　　　　of Berberophone womanhood.

The phalanx of the gnarled Mother ones
Swirling like gnats in a dust swollen myth
　　　Billowing in sunless effusion
as leaden-black snowflakes
　　Settling throughout the gut-hewn hut
of scorched dust
and yogurt billage.
　　Anointed by fresh vomit.

 In breath-stippled syncopation
　　　　We moved to the scream strewn straw.

　　　　　　　... three scorpions scampered ...
Over frozen hemp sandals
on crucified soles and
　　　　　Western obtundent eyes.
Benumbed blankness.
Feigning understanding.
While obsidian cataracts
　　　damned.

　　　Oh, the screaming had never abated.
　　　　For her mother
　　　　For the fervid hands that bound her

For the storm of black snowflakes
             That pried her innocent labia
                While the Ancient One
                   Flicked bone skewer
                      Criss-cross, Criss-cross
                         The sacred

whet stone.
             I thought it would be quick
             Like some cutting room castoff bit
                         of documentarian vagaries.
But no.
It was not.
                ...such a tiny clitoris...

And with each deft puncture of
That
Pearlescent
Infant Vagina
             New shrieks were born.

                From what can neither be forgiven
                      Nor forgotten.

                   Witness
                  'Scholar'
                            Field researching
             Accomplice.

Agonistes mistress
Tortured unto death.

Previously published in *Neonbeam*, *The Rat* and in Erbacce Press Chapbook, *Sublunary Curse*.

Clinical, Brutal....

Cancer Puff Piece

Constance Stadler

Fucking brilliant.

Something
Inside of you
Conspires
To kill you.

Who else but a loving
Merciful, gentle Lord
Could come up
With such a perfect plan?

One fish feeds
Thousands
One cell breeds millions

And then comes

The tubes and the burning
The ritual retching
The follicle cascade
The wheelchairs on parade
Blue pan/green band
Eviscerate, Evaporate
Flesh   coated   sheets

Shrinking and waning
Shrieking and waiting

Morphine drip
Have mercy on us

I had a love
He was tall
He was fair
He was brilliant

He was gentle

But you didn't care.

Originally published by *Luciole Press*, also in eBook *Paper Cuts* (Calliope Nerve).

Clinical, Brutal....

THE BASTARDIZER (Excerpt)

Bill Thunder

Something was niggling me when I arrived back at the office. I was a little out of breath from the walk. Not because I'm out of shape, but because the combination of high humidity – sitting at a stagnant treacle-like 90% – and alveoli-clogging pollution hanging heavy in the air made it harder to draw and absorb oxygen. I daresay the three cigarettes I'd smoked on the way hadn't helped much. I was sweating profusely: it was no cooler outside than in that sauna of an interview room they'd spent three hours and 12 minutes grilling me. I also needed to piss. The coffee had gone through my system and had filled by bladder to its full 800ml capacity. Fully distended and with the fluids contained therein creating an almost unbearable pressure, I had crossed the 150ml – 300ml point of micturation some time ago.

I leaned back and eased the door open with just the tip of my boot. It swung slowly, silently in its hinges. Silence. Perhaps I'd been mistaken after all. Perhaps in my haste – in being hustled out, I'd forgotten to close the door properly and to lock up. Unlikely.

Cautiously, I crossed the threshold, scanning left, right – as far right as the door, still only half-open would allow – and straight ahead. The place had been turned over. In broad daylight, too! Not that there was much to turn. This is precisely why I keep everything of potential interest stored off premises. Still silence. Looks like I've missed the intruder.

Still, I proceed with caution and enter fully. The desk drawers have been jimmied open and their contents – a few invoices for telephone, electricity and the like for the office, a couple of spare notebooks, business cards (mostly my own plus a few for taxi firms and so on) are scattered about on the tiled floor. The PC's on and has been left open at the 'My documents' panel. As if I'd be so dumb as to leave anything anyone might want in there. Either the intruder got spooked or otherwise got bored having realised there was nothing to be got from this place.

Just then, I heard something. A slight creak. The toilet door? I spun round and caught the side of a man's face peering out to see if the coast was clear. Clearly he'd not been banking on me standing between him and the exit.

In three long, fast strides, I was at the back of the office and at the lavatory door. He instinctively slammed it shut. What was he going to do, stay locked in my toilet till I got bored and went away? I met the door with my shoulder and powered it open with the force of my fill body weight, 188.5lbs.

The door swung back and made full contact with his chest and chin, throwing him backwards where he collided with the wall directly behind him. The room was a mere 3' across. He simultaneously caught the right ilium of his pelvis against the washbasin with a dull thud. An expression of pain flickered across his face and I was on him instantly, landing a sharp blow to the stomach. The air rushed from his lungs like a paper bag being burst and he doubled over just as I raised my knee. It connected with his face and there was a resounding crack as his left nasal bone shattered into the pulpy matter of his lower lateral cartilages and septum. He howled with pain and snapped his head back up, blood spurting from his nostrils and spraying the off-white walls and crisp white tiles on the floor.

He lunged forward blindly and I tried to side-step his wild flailing blows but there isn't room in this confined space and he caught the side of my head with the knuckles his large light hand, balled into a fist.

Trying to take advantage of this brief respite from my initial onslaught, he makes to barge past me, out into the office. He's halfway through the door when I stick my foot out – a simple but effective move that lands his flat on his face, half in and half out of the minuscule WC.

He groans and has turned himself half over by the time I'm on him, his collars bunched up in my fists.

'Who the fuck are you?' I demand, flecks of spittle spraying from my mouth and onto his face. I can be an animal when I'm angry or threatened. Right now, I was both. I drive a punch into his mouth. The look on his face tells me that his pain receptors are overloading in response to the blow I had just landed him. I plant another in this throat and can almost see his trachea inflaming instantaneously.

'Fuck you,' he snarls breathlessly through gritted teeth that are red with blood from his nose. He jerks his neck in a wild attempt to headbutt me, but I manage to roll my torso off to one side while keeping his legs pinned with my own.

'Look, you little fucker,' I growl, you're gonna talk. Who sent you?' He's a nasty-looking bastards and anything but little: thick-set, burly, at least 250lbs of pumped-up bulk, and well over 6' tall. He's fucking ugly to boot: his beady eyes are close together and set under the crags of a low forehead and knitted eyebrows. His head's shaven, too. Standard hired muscle. Generic bouncer type. I'd never spot him in an ID parade of meatheads who stand outside pubs and clubs in black coats on a Friday or Saturday night.

'I'm not telling you shit,' he pants as he wriggles and struggles to loosen my grip.

'Tell me!' I demand.

'No!'

'Tell me!' I repeat, louder this time.

'No!'

'Tell me!'

'No!'

'Tell me!' I'm practically screaming in his face now. I'm foaming at the mouth and set my eyes in a manic stare, adopting the methods of the Anglo-Saxon berserkers.

'Speak or you'll regret it,' I snarl.

'Fuck you,' he growls in response.

I land a heavy punch right in his mouth, neatly removing his lower right bicuspid which tumbles onto the floor and skitters across the tiles, resting in a small tarn of plasma and platelets. In striking this blow I sustain a nick to my second knuckle. It's deep and saliva-filled and stings like hell. What's more, the force of the strike throws me off balance and he manages to land a hook to my larynx. I'm winded and struggling for air and he slips out from beneath me.

My hypothalamic-pituitary-adrenal axis suddenly goes into overdrive, powering waves of adrenaline through my system. Supercharged, I renew my attack on my assailant with new-found vigour, a boot connecting with his testes, evincing a howl of pain.

Before I know it, he's on his feet and brandishing a knife while I'm incapacitated, on my hands and knees. He's coming for me, and draws his foot back to land a boot in my ribs, but I manage to roll myself out of the way and he connects with nothing but air. I take advantage of his being off balance and swing my leg round, skittling his weight-bearing and weaker left leg from under him. He lands on the floor flat on his back. It's a heavy sound and the knife rattles across the ground.

He makes a strange elongated enunciation of pain on impact and I'm able to raise myself to my feet and jab him hard in the kidney. I'm about to pin him to the ground with his face to the tiles, make him taste the floor, when he jabs an elbow back and catches me square in the jaw with it.

With remarkable deftness for such an unwieldy hulk, the thug springs up and is out of the door before I can regain my feet. I can hear the clatter of his footsteps receding as I haul myself up. There's no point trying to give chase. He's gone.

Battered and pissed off, I lug myself to the window and see him racing across the street before disappearing into the early rush-hour crowds.

I flip the bird in his general direction out of the window.

'Bastard,' I curse, rubbing my sore jaw ruefully.

Fucking pussy couldn't finish what he'd started, and wouldn't stick around to give me the pleasure either. I'd've taken him apart given the opportunity.

It's no good, I have to urinate. I move to the toilet, unzip my fly, unleash my manhood and piss hard for 2 minutes and 49 seconds. I exhale, a long, long sigh of relief. The release of pressure as the hot jet of urine arcs into the bowl is nigh on orgasmic. I finish, shake off, wash my hands and head back into the main office. I need to clean the blood off the walls and floor at some point, but right now there's work to do.

Clinical, Brutal....

You Ain't Foolin' Me

David Mark Dannov

Tampon commercials

crack me up.

They're so soft

and feminine

and show sunlight through pink curtains

and wonderfully clean bedspreads;

and the women are beautiful

and their hair is perfectly curled,

their faces made up—

everything

so grand

and full of family outings

      and the wagging

      of a dog's tail.

      How ridiculous!

I mean,

if you cut through the bullshit,

what they're really talking about

is blood,

lots of stinky-ass blood

that comes out of the vagina.

Isn't that right, girls?

The Assassin

David Mark Dannov

I was working in a bar
when this old man sat down and introduced himself.
He had sparkling black eyes,
wearing a 40's worn-rimmed hat.
He reminded me of William Boroughs.
I asked him what he did for a living.

"I'm retired," he smiled.

"No, before you retired."

"You don't want to know."

"Sure I do. What'd you do, kill people
for a living?"

He hesitated a moment. "Yes."

"Yes what?"

"I killed people for a living.
I was a hired assassin." He said that without blinking.
"I've murdered 130 people. At least."

"Really," I smirked, not quite believing him.
"How'd you do it, mostly?"

"I used a poison on people's steering wheels."

I looked at him
and got a cold chill.

Clinical, Brutal....

Solid as a Rock

Christopher Bateman

Certain phrases amuse me on account of their absurdity. Other terms – particularly in the corporate world – annoy me simply because they're so meaningless. So, as I was engrossed in a hard morning's chairpounding (well, the mortgage doesn't pay itself), my attention was – as is often the case – cut through with random snippets of conversation from those around me, with occasional phrases standing out from the general babble.

'So can I use this phone or not?'

'Yes.'

'But why can't I log into it?'

'It's a soft phone.'

We're all on soft phones now.

Now, I understand – but abhor – the 'soft' prefix, but generally understand the concept. Software isn't hardware, it isn't physical. Hence 'soft skills' aren't physical, don't have form, aren't concrete.

The telephone on my desk, however, didn't look very abstract to me. Extending my hand toward the object before me, I was able to affirm what I had known before: it had a physical form. I poked the large lump of moulded grey plastic, with buttons and an LCD screen, that sat before me on my desk. It too is supposed to be a soft phone. But it isn't remotely soft. In fact, it's as hard as any other hefty chunk of moulded plastic stuffed with wires and circuitry and a speaker.

I hoisted it from the desk top, and hefted it in my hand. It's not only hard, but heavy. But I needed proof.

The dumb corporate-babbling bimbo was still prattling on about systems and extensions and logging in. I'd heard enough. I'd had enough, and launched the thing in my hand toward her head.

The object met with her cranium with a sickening thud. There was a high-pitched shriek of agony as she fell to the floor, followed a split second later by a loud clatter as the telephony device crashed to the ground, its LCD cracked but otherwise largely intact.

A trickle of blood ran from the dent in the bint's head, an ultra-livid bruise forming around it before my eyes. The phone was, as I had believed all along, quite unsoft: in fact, it was particularly hard, and without doubt harder than her skull.

'Fucking corporate bollocks,' I grumbled as I swung my chair back around and resumed my work.

Clinical, Brutal....

The Quest Part 4. Strange Connections: Jack Harris' Funeral

Simon Phillips

Well over the weekend mum phoned to tell me that Jack Harris had died a victim of this summer's heatwave, as his heart couldn't take it after he had a fall and the treatment on his injured leg caused a heart attack.

Jack is or was and always will be an old friend of the family as his parents lived in the same tenement in Flower and Dean Street in Whitechapel, the flowery as it was better known, or as my nanna Lily used to pronounce it Floradine St. Then when the families got bombed out during the blitz they both ended up in Pembury Road Hackney on The Pembury Estate they lived there in Claremont house with the Phillips on the ground floor and the Harris' above them.

Jack fought in Burma and managed to survive, he was quite well known as a singer and did all sorts of other stuff. He always used to tell me that the first time he met me I was still in Mum's stomach and she was about 3 months pregnant by that time. He is also one of the only non family members that ever talked to me about being at my bris!! My first actual memory of meeting Jack must be from about 1968 or 69, I'd have been 3 or 4 years old and I was along with Andrew staying for the weekend or at least Friday night with nanna Mill on the Pembury and at some point during the time we spent there nanna Mill took us upstairs to see Jack and Bobbie, his wife of it turned out some 57 years in the end, who were round at his parents place, I think his parents were still alive then, I'm really not sure it is too hazy a memory that has flooded back since I heard the bad news.

I don't really recall anything else about it though, but I do have a strong memory of going up to see them on more than one occasion. I'm also pretty sure Jack was about on the day in May of 1974 that we helped Nanna Mill move out of the Pembury and over to St Johns Wood. But let's skip back in time again a little bit as according to Mum Jack and Bobby really helped her out when my namesake Simon Phillips died in October 1962. As back then my brother Andrew was all of 3 months old, and mum just didn't know how she was going to cope trying to support dad and the rest of the family through this tragedy of Simon dying aged 54, which also happened to be the number on the door of mum and dad's house.

Well Jack suggested that if she could get hold of a spare carry cot or crib then He and Bobby would look after Andrew all week while mum was downstairs in the Shiva house helping to get everyone through the week. So that then all mum had to manage every day was to get from home in Redbridge by train and bus to Hackney every day, as dad was leaving for the Shiva much earlier than her. This was act of kindness that I know mum has never forgotten and is still thankful for.

Over the years Jack has been at just about every family funeral I can remember on Dad's side of the family and also at just about all the weddings and Bar Mitzvahs. He also used to sit further along the pew to us in Shul and was always full of jokes and little wind-ups in a similar way to dad.

So yesterday I went over and had lunch with mum and then we went round to Jack and Bobbie's place in Redbridge not that far from Mum's.

And after we had expressed our regrets with Bobbie and her kids and Grand-kids of whom I only recognised the son, I drove mum and some of Jack's family out to Rainham for the funeral. Once we were out there I went for a walk with mum to visit Dad and also Nanna Mill and Simon, and then to Nanna Lily and Marks (pronounced Max). And we had to say our hello's to a few more people besides with the customary hello to Fay Handworker whoever she was.

Then when we got back to outside the chapel I ran into Joyce Brent who also came out of The Pembury and ended up in Redbridge Lane East, and she introduced me to the man she was with as Adam's friend. That was a bit of a jolt to me, as her son Adam died in 1977 or 78 in what must have been September or maybe early October when he dived head first into the shallow end at the Lido and never made it out of the pool again. This was a truly shocking event in my childhood as I had been playing round with Adam the day before and he had been boasting of how they were going to go to the Lido in the afternoon after going to Shul in the morning, as if memory serves me right it was Succous, so we were off school in term time. Although I can't recall for certain now, I'm pretty sure I would have chatted with Adam in Shul during the morning as well. But Adam knew that my mum was far too orthodox to let me go swimming on Yom-Tov in case anyone saw us doing something we weren't meant to. I can still remember walking down the road with mum and Andrew and Dad to go to the Shiva and the house was packed and Jack and Joyce Brent sat there shaking in disbelief, no one knew how to comfort them.

So that all these 25 or so years later it is still a painful memory for Joyce and I know just thinking about Adam has brought tears to my eyes, knowing how hard it has been for Joyce and Jack to live on knowing their only son died so young.

The funeral also gave me my first chance to see our new rabbi in action he did pretty well as the service ran smoothly and we all followed the coffin out onto the parched grounds and back once more into the chapel for the Kaddish. A good turn out then all wished Bobbie and the kids and Jack's brother Long life and we then took the slow drive back to Redbridge. I'm sure had I been with dad he would have introduced me to all sorts of characters from the past, but that wasn't to be.

Well Jack sorry to see you go I'm sure you will be missed by lots of family and friends and all of those that you touched with your acts of generosity or your jokes and singing.

Clinical, Brutal....

Picturehouse Blues

Maria Gornell

An air of trembling doubt
Clicks in heels on hollowed
Substance users streets
Where capital of culture's
Failure wallows in instant
Gratification; the face of poverty
Has no heroes.

On this side of town
Dilapidated buildings
Stand forlorn weeping
For a London road

Once busy bustling
thriving with business
Investment and life.

Now home
To pushers, peddlers
Outside on fringes underclass
Piss and cum stained streets
Stench of beer and smoke

Spaced out teenagers

Roaming with pit bull dogs
Ready to attack.

A £1 a pint bar
Fully equipped with
Poker room for addicts
Old working class man's
Manifesto vomited with lies
Out of work

Eyeing us with suspicion
Mocking individuality
Hardened by ignorance
In leather faced scorn.

Soon outnumbered by
Our visions of creative
Collective inclusion.

It was time
To step out of comfort zones.
Unsteady steps into unknown
As the night washed over us

Broken hearts can sob
Only so long

Before the fire returns

Clinical, Brutal....

Burning with desires

To let go
Taking this town by storm
The planets excited raging
Beside human resilience

A once worn out diva
Poet
Guitarist
spectator

Singing the blues
Purging distant ghosts
singing for freedom

Soon the bar is heaving
With sounds of samba
Spanish guitars and
Drum beats to vibration
Of earth.

A little man takes the floor
Bending arching back
Awakening a fire repressed
In every throbbing vein.

As the heavens open with

Pure cleansing rain.

We remember to howl.

Clinical, Brutal....

<u>Rise</u>

Maria Gornell

i. Citizenship

Post fascism

Digs its heels

In deep

Capitalism coils

Many sleep blind

Apathetic ghosts

Seduced with consumerism

As the world turns clockwise

Death knells in west

Sunrise

'Viva revolution'

Fragments of proletariat rebels

Die screaming

Under an indifferent sky

Hypnotised by popular culture

Torn between ancestor cries

And instant gratification

Lines of static words

Oblique letter lies

Citizenship weapon

Of mass destruction

Crumble our resolve.

ii Enlightenment

I stop only
To inhale deeply
Fresh summer scent air
Cleansed with rivers
Of rain.
Wild woman heart
Beats faster
Palms appear messy
Many paths to choose.
I choose no longer
To hide in shady
Overgrowth
Instead I sparkle
In uncertain times
Enlightenment arrives
Magic is in the air.
I soak in its wonder
Dance in its transformative
Power
My aura lights the dusk
Reflected against trees
Infinite sky
Leaves rustling

Clinical, Brutal....

Through winds

Carrying whispers

Of reason on earth.

I hum soft harmonies

Blending in nature

Feeling love all around me

Consoling self

Do not be afraid

A new age has dawned

Ingenious arise

Breathing deeply

I anticipate

Only the soft cry

Of spiritual freedom

Citizen of universe

Rise.

Into the Earth

Christopher Nosnibor

...a tumult of flesh, bodies piled up on top of one another in an endless seething mass, writhing, teeming... fermenting, a foment, torment, a throbbing, seething miasma, a formless, disorganised mess of disconnected body parts, entangled and ungainly; hair, teeth, limbs, eyes, mouths, torsos. The whole tower is unstable and looks as though it may topple at any moment... Welcome to the human carnival, a carnival of the grotesque, a procession of freaks, unique and disturbing, one and all. It's an endless train of bodies of all shapes and sizes, and here, in this microcosm, I find myself hemmed in amongst them, a scared observer trapped in the midst of the carny parade of bearded children, cyclopses, lumbering giants, screaming cadavers, the living dead, and near-lithic hulks of flesh, mountainous beings, deformed and distorted, rippling rolls of flesh, aprons hanging down over their shrivelled and shrunken nether regions, deprived of air or light. They clamber over one another in their eternal quests for food, space, seats, storage for their luggage, bouncing to and fro, lugging their devolved and degenerated carcasses with great difficulty, rubbing shoulder to shoulder with one another. It's every man, woman and child for themselves. There is no end.

...and so it goes on. And on, relentlessly, mercilessly. This is not some finely-honed machine, pulsating hearts and respiring lungs and skin and secreting glands working in unison for the same unified end. There is no extrinsic, universal or even wider commonality, no synchronisation, no organisation, no coordination. Instead of harmony, it's anarchy, a riot of cells, unruly and uncoordinated, disjointed and disconnected, dissociated, spreading and multiplying and growing with no concept and no concern for the long-term outcome, namely an explosion not only of population in broader terms, but, more immediately, an explosion of living breathing tissue – meat, muscle, bone and intestinal tract, heart lungs livers kidneys, cartilage and gristle, pancreas and sinews, nerves and floating clots drifting down overwrought corpuscles and narrow, clogged salt-filled, fat-lined channels; nerves, frayed and begging for mercy, gonads, subcutaneous fats, pigments, ovaries, hair, skin and undifferentiated tissue, mutated cancerous cells etc, all cosseted in layer upon layer of fat, fetid, yellow, thick and putrid. And the aroma of it all! The scent of sweat, of stale urine, of decaying flesh, the stench of humanity, packed into a confined space.

No milk of human kindness here, just the incessant gurgling of intestinal fluids, the slurping of syrupy drinks from plastic cups through straws and the splash of piss and excrement in uneasy colons and brimming bladders. It's no easy ride, and while man may be a social animal, when forced into close – uncomfortably, tightly-packed, hemmed-in close – proximity with fellow humans – strangers – for a protracted period of time, those social tendencies are more likely to manifest themselves as borderline sociopathic tendencies. Empathy dissolves as every passenger fights for their seat, their space, the safety of their own luggage, the last sandwich on the mobile refreshments trolley, the last piece of toilet paper in the flooding shared facilities that they have had to queue outside for half an hour while someone selfish dithers over their defecation and then proceeds to leave the pipe half-blocked and the tap running.

And so the hiccoughing aggravation begins, and it's anything but pretty. The gnashing of teeth, the heavy sighs, the gasping, the wheezing, the huffing and puffing, the foaming at the mouth: these are the sounds that permeate the air and congeal with the clamorous chatter of conversation, the ringing of mobile telephones, the hissing of cans of lager and pop being opened and poured down the gullets of an ever fattening nation. The sounds, the smells of the fetid blubber, the blocked and streaming glands, the digestive juices, bubbling volcanically, rumbling in the depths of the land-whales are dank, unsettling, somehow unnatural, but all too natural, and all too real.

The scene is repeated endlessly on lines across the nation: this journey is in no way special. This particular train ride simply represents a microcosm of the broader society. Western civilisation. Global civilisation. Each man – and woman, child, being of indeterminate gender – is an island. Each island possesses its own infrastructure, the biological mechanisms keeping each island functioning, but how efficiently? Each island differs, but one thing is clear: across these islands, there is a continent-wide crisis. The land masses – these fragmented, fractured pieces of land, floating on the infinite sea of life – are slowly sinking. They're overpopulated, congested, badly polluted. The consumption is unsustainable in the long term.

But the governments of these islands, which have all declared independence from one another, are oblivious, or otherwise simply unwilling to act. Each individual – the term being applied loosely, as each very much resembles another, or, indeed, almost all of the others – is thus a microcosm, a micro-labyrinth within a global labyrinth, which exists as but a speck of dust in the cosmic scheme, the infinite labyrinth which extends far beyond the conception of anyone on this sinking raft.

There is a mid-range hum – the babble of empty conversation about clothes, shopping, stocks and shares, business meetings, lunches, parties, domestic issues and arrangements, he said she said I said and it was like and I was going and it's incessant, never-ending, and relentlessly inane, facile, purposeless, beyond filling the silence... but there is never silence. Never a second passes in pure, perfect silence. Just for a moment, try to actually imagine true silence. It's impossible. There's also a high-end conglomeration of sounds: the air conditioning, the wind as it rushes down the length of the carriages, cut through by the aerodynamically shaped engine as it races forwards, the scrape of metal against metal as the wheels grind in circular contact with the tracks... and to complete the frequency spectrum, there is the dull roar of the engine and, barely audible but just, jut there, just discernible in the hubbub and racketous clamour of Everything Else, the deep, dark pulsating rumblings of blood circulating – a tide of pulses, a sea of blood, all coming together – pulsating organs. Organs coated in a thick layer of yellow fat, choking, struggling against the odds and against biology to function, to sustain the host. It's a losing battle, a seething mass of free-floating cholesterols, carotid arteries, furred lungs and sluggish thyroid glands. Tired, enlarged hearts pumping, working overtime and on the brink of explosion.

Outside, the sky darkens rapidly: from deep blue smudged with traces of blackness like soot, before becoming engulfed by treacle, running down descending in a matter of minutes to smother the land.... but this journey will go on forever, not only here, but the world over, until the world ends or humanity ceases to exist.

Clinical, Brutal....

LOVE COLLIDES AND NOTHING IS PERMITTED?
The Director's Cut of
Love Collides and Nothing is Prohibited:

Lee Kwo

There is an abstract pattern of neo-cortical warfare and the warning that you can never capture the embodied actuality unless it is as prolix and noisy as the body itself dying in yr arms cold life threatening head noise of drained memory riding euphoric ridges realized without intention a refuge of patterns of informational corrosion seeking the random mouth precipitating innocence under control of instantiation sensual and over determined by sheer volume of silence a double adaptor floating in time as exposed passage where order emerges out of violation for there is only imagination outside of techne and the plenitude of music filled with beginnings not knowing where to end thought travels made mobile by sound from one glottal assemblage to the other Unica starts to make sense surrounded by her particles of anonymous matter she speaks under decay of non pulsed signs her mess-ages of meaning aroused and salvaged from estrangement just enough time to achieve exhaustion or fatigue in split second mobility of inertia I wait for you to move she says smoke that cigarette she asks what the ear can observe unable to close itself how jealous it is of the eye oh what a plethora of dialects you compose yr verbal drifts across its destiny a devouring innovation of the enigmatic gaping holes of black necrotic digressions breaking thru the cerebral she hits degree zero and lets the step to monologue be taken by the lungs she would believe in the last liquid soul of rituals and to see the whole by means of the part this oppressive sense of transience a desire of contiguity for continuity a lust that cannot be satisfied catastrophe slows down the surest sign of the passage violence in its final appearance to be come inertial to the point of living in slow motion of living for nothing and nothing to live for Unica is not a mere empirical accident but a pathological extravagance whose natural companions are poverty and ill health Chroma fluids and Blue Saturn shattered nerves and inhibitions pains without history imitation of the fugitive departure of the passionate embrace of systematic confusion oh how Unica yearns for the old meta-physical sensory phenomena of critical paranoia of excrement blood and putrefaction reality strives painfully to imitate appearance a simple moral act a complicated unmotivated act keeps going to the limits of endurance she cut out the mouth of someone once loved but seen no more she remained a few moments stunned as if asleep weeping as when one turns on a switch there is often darkness in a pool of vibrating gravity and solitude those who love are like celestial bodies radiating splendour aching for somnambulance and the joys of revenge are not to be exercised with out punishment a ritualised enactment of the moment we lost control of our machines an endless circulation of ghostly emotions drove Unica to the edge of the abyss voyeurs search a space in which the body is a terminal transitory point a secret about a secret nullifying explanation the other of sense the origin of non-sense where the proximity of silence and noise is hear synchronistically Unicas noise has the meaning you give to it she speaks ruthless anachronistic the circus of hysteria is disintegrating attests to the virulence of the fatality of being a conduit of superficiality for the sake of being different she says I take my self seriously after 3am riding the infernal clamour of the airwaves/n schizophrenic meaning and paranoid violence the phases of the moon extort their damage of all the senses vision is the coldest and most distant She says no there is nothing I have lost that I could not afford to replace a mouthful of endurance first of all the compulsion to abstract negation torn from the primitive and complex vibrating on the margins of a theoretical swamp of bodily extrusions a wrenched nde a bruised rib and depression is seductive because it attains a point of saturation leasving behind documents that Raw solitude hitting the wall of post verbal transition so many anegoric deliriums that keep me awake at night the sewn up body of circulating thought the masochist can only hear but never speak the instructions must be obeyed/thought turned machinic in the darkness of schizo-paranoia the walls are moving ceiling torn open by the clouds the traffic is at a dead stop the birds have no wings the vivid shit exalts the dead corpse eats into own viscera and the noise of the moaning is an attempt to introduce disorder into the system of dying/ Gestaltungen collapsing into the NOW of the future which leaks out always finding the horror of one more day one more night unbearable in its indiscretion the infernal bodies of death mess and wreckage/The lone DogMan is an OutLaw a bizarreness of solitary confinement hunting down the accomplice/the insomniac has no dreams but only nightmare fantasies of dreams /a dark bloody sense of the erotic/ Can actions dissolve the way words disappear?/ I wander in the excessive plenitude of the jammed lithium frequencies of body in motion mind flatlined/ May all yr nights be surreal and all yr days Dada/

The Battlefield of Carnivores

Pablo Vision

When you die you become all people. You have done everything that has been done. You have said everything that has been said. You return to the collective oneness from which you came. You are everything that has been, and everything that will be. But this is not paradise found, and this is not Hell eternal: this is something much more dreadful. This is all the evil, the sickness, the atrocity, the injustice, the pain, and the madness – but seen from the terrible perspective of sanity. There is no relief, and there is no oblivion. There is nowhere to run to, but much to run from. And there are no gods.

But that is when you die.

For now we are all madmen on the run; running away from all the horror in the here and now; and we must find solace wherever we can, and in whatever way that we can.

**

I killed a man with my bare hands, because I needed to commit a crime for which I would be punished. I confessed to another crime, so that the killer would remain free, and so that he could take life again. But I am no recidivist – even sucking at the tit, I was thinking, "Fuck me, mother,

183

fuck me." And without irony, or lack thereof, the man I killed was my own father.

When I was young I burned the books of Nietzsche because I thought there were no absolute truths; I ate the ashes because there are no absolute lies; I shat it all out because the truth does not lie in-between, and because Nietzsche, as we all know, abhors a vacuum. I pissed on Darwin, and I masturbated over the Bible.

When I was younger still, I pulled the legs off insects, one at a time, to see how they would endure; I cut off my own nipple to see if it would grow back; I set fire to my school just to watch the flames.

I killed my father many times: I smashed his head to a pulp, with a stone that I held in both hands; I ripped his still beating heart from his chest; I cut off his cock, and rammed it down his throat, until he chocked; I skinned him alive, so that he slowly haemorrhaged to death; I stuck him with knives, and fucked these holes until my cock was sore. I cannot recall with certainty which way I killed him, but this seems the most vivid: my hands around his frail neck, squeezing until the life left his pleading, bulging eyes. And when it was over I kissed him, tenderly on the forehead; glad to have delivered him from pain, for I did not know then, what torment I was sending him to. And then I kissed his mouth, just to know what it felt like.

I was doomed from the moment the sperm entered my mother's cunt, and the destiny that was passed on from the first heterotrophic Adam that crawled out of the slime, and into the pus of humanity. And then I absorbed the sickness of the world around me like osmosis.

At first I cared, and then I cared less and less. The infinity of thought, and the absence of resolution, overwhelmed me. The attempts to reconcile the irreconcilable made me sick. I can no longer be sure what things I have done, and what things I have imagined doing. I am unable to distinguish dreams from memories. My attempts to document my thoughts in moments of relative clarity are thwarted by my uncertainty over what actually constitutes *reality*. I find long lists of unpunctuated sentences, in my own hand, that I have no recollection of writing.

I have recall of tenderness and sacrifice, kindness and love. I can remember moments of pure joy. But all of this is punctuated with acts of extreme violence, and obsession with excrement. That these acts and obsessions went mostly unpunished, and unfound, must give testimony to some sort of normality.

Perhaps I was just too fragile to survive in this battlefield of carnivores. Perhaps my complete inability to empathise with the rest of humanity caused this conflict between compassion and abhorrence. And no drug or faith could obliterate this feeling of being crushed under the weight of atrocity, or the need to strike out in equal measure. No distraction could completely placate or subdue the perversity and obscenity of the thoughts that bombarded me.

I have difficulty concentrating, but I write when I can. I fear that I will never be able to assemble any of this into coherency. If it is of any benefit at all, it is for my own. It is a communication to my future self; a self that is becoming evermore disintegrated and fragmented.

The thoughts that rush through my mind are too many and too confused to make any kind of sense of. They are often images: a box of wire framed glasses, taken from the bodies of gassed Jews; the cunts of young girls being mutilated by their own mothers; two young boys inserting batteries up the anus of a younger boy, and cutting off his fingers with scissors; burning villages and mushroom clouds; cells mutating and spreading; niggers hanging from trees; women burning at the stake, women impaled in Judas Cradles, women buried to the head in Iranian soil, and being stoned to death, and liberated Vietnamese women being raped by American soldiers; box-cutters, mobile phones, planes, and the collapsing carcasses of buildings; humans with pig-like flesh and strings of shit trailing from their behinds, like entrails; and mounds and mounds and mounds of corpses.

And these images are persistent and insistent. And the half-thoughts that surround these images are often just as confusing, but if there is any conclusion at all, it is that these atrocities are not limited to geography, a time in history, power and corruption, religion, or culture, but that they are universal: it is our very nature. If there is any argument for this illusion of civilisation and progress, then the actuality of it is without reason, and without reason there is madness. I am unable to make the small transactions of mutual benefit with others. I am unable to turn off my mind and opiate myself in the vacuity of distraction. And I am unable to come to terms with the impotency of not being able to eradicate these things, from the world, and from my mind. I have seen the attempts others have made, and have only seen one tyranny replaced with another.

So although this is a communication to myself, I am aware that others will read it; the mind of one madman, in a world full of madness, is, I find, surprisingly interesting to others. I will not apologise for dragging you through the sewage of humanity, and rubbing your nose into the excrement of life, for it is your choice to read these words, and furthermore, it offers a taste of all that you will see in the hereafter. Make your own choices as to what is real and what is not real. Make your futile attempts to order this, and try and establish reason, if you feel that you must. I care little what you do.

I will write again, when, and only if, I am able to do so.

About the contributors.

Christopher Bateman exists in the realm of the third mind between Christopher Nosnibor and Stewart Bateman. As such, s/he does not exist in the physical sense or occupy a space in the concrete world. S/He does, however, emerge when the time and mood is right and is greater than the sum of his/her parts.

Stuart Bateman wastes most of his time as a wage slave, but occasionally gets to indulge his passion for multimedia art. He co-authored *C.N.N.* with Christopher Nosnibor in 2007 and assisted in establishing Clinicality Press later the same year. He lives in Leeds and likes to photograph building sites, demolition sites and scaffolding.

Carl van Cleave applies the cut-up technique and a number of internet-based programs in the formulation of his experimental poetry, and literally to the brain. He is fascinated by emerging technologies, developing methods of communication, telepathy, pornography, philosophy, avant-gardism and the Marquis de Sade. He lives at home with his mother's mutilated corpse.

Vincent Clasper should probably get out more. Unfortunately reality and other people interfere with his cognitive processes. He lives in various places, often relying on the kindness of the few friends he does have for places to crash, dividing his time between London, Edinburgh, Oslo, Vienna and New York. Mostly, though, he lives in his own head and is currently single.

David Mark Dannov graduated with a creative writing degree from CSULB in 1994. He was a waiter, a commercial painter, a landscaper, a pizza delivery driver, a valet, a caterer, a plant tech, a gardener, a rehabilitation specialist, and a substitute teacher. He's been published by *Chiron Review* and *Outside Writers* as a featured poet, including *Pearl*, *Tears in the Fence*, *Edit Red*, *Emerging Edge Publishing*, *Poet Plant Press*, *The Poetry Warrior*, *Bottle of Smoke Press*, *Black Spring Press*, *Black Cross Magazine*, *Hay Wire Press*, *The Brown Bottle*, *Peaky Hide*, and several other poetry magazines. In 1999, he won the Lucid Moon Poetry Contest for a poem entitled 'There Are So Many Canyons And Valleys In The Skin Of An Orange.' Two excerpts from his novel, *Awake* were published in a Paul Krassner book entitled *Mushrooms and Other Highs, Toad Slime to Ecstasy*, which came out in 2003. David's first chapbooks of poems, *There Are Poets Who Live Amongst The Dead, Wanted Dead or Alive and Inhuman* were published by Black Joke Press in 2006; a full length poetry book *It's the Shaking of the Ground that Crumbles Walls but Doesn't Crumble Trees* is now available on Black Joke Press, including his newest poetry books, *Notes of an Ordinary Man Held Captive in an Alien World* and *The Crack in the Sidewalk Speaks*. Inkwater Press will publish his children's novel in 2009 under a pseudonym.

David currently lives in with his girlfriend in Long Beach. He paints, sculpts, and is involved in several music projects.

Jock Drummond was born in Glasgow in 1969, where he almost died at birth through strangulation with his own umbilical cord. Having survived this and various other traumas, he grew up to work in various menial jobs, from dock-work to admin in the city centre. At the turn of the millennium he left for London, where he has since worked in various menial admin jobs and has, more recently, turned his hand to writing. He admires Christopher Brookmyre's work, but is confident that his own is better, and likes to watch *CSI* and *NCIS* in what little spare time he has. He lives with his third wife, Clarissa, and their three children, who he hopes will never read anything he's written.

Kestra Fay has always been something of a flounderer, regularly beginning and rarely completing. Published a little, some years ago, reviewing bands for AAA gig entry and free CDs – don't knock it till you've tried it.

Maria Gornell is published in Shoots and Vines all female anthology 'I Can Not be Your Virgin Mother,' and issue 1 as well as featured online zines *Counterexample Poetics, The Beat, Debris Magazine, Black-Listed Magazine, Lit Up Magazine, Covert Poetics, Heroin Love Songs, Opium Poetry, Agua* issue 1 Scintillating Publication, *Liverpool 800* anthology and *Heartbeats* journal. She lives in Liverpool where she is training in counselling and works in group therapy.

Radcliff Gregory: Author of *Everywhere, Except...,* and the sold-out *Fragile Art,* and *Figaro's Cabin* (under a pseudondym), and also anthologised in *Chroma, Poemata, Coffee House* and *Poets International* literary publications, and a dozen books by publishers including Crystal Clear, Forward Press and Poetry Now. Outright winner of six UK poetry competitions. Also writes non-fiction articles and essays on literary criticism, literature, disability and gender issues. Currently organising Polyverse Poetry Festival, which he founded. He also tries to find time to complete his first full-length prose work.

S F Grimm: Born in 1976 in Canada to wealthy but unloving parents, he was expelled from seven private schools in four continents by the age of 12 – mostly for fighting, but occasionally for writing shockingly offensive essays. After dropping out of university, he began writing works that eventually influenced Clinical Brutality after becoming convinced that Descartes was in error concerning the existence of himself – but not of others. After a long battle with Alcoholism, and a short stint at Her Majesty's pleasure for committing a string of crimes that were not so much petty as trivial, he developed his fusion of Ayer and Quine inspired radically pragmatic scepticism which he has termed 'loose-tight solipsism.' His literary work is a 'sci-art' – a syncretic combination of post-Deriddian multi-authoring techniques and a Žižekian deconstruction of the language of morality – essentially expressing his 'non self' through texts that render the reader both the actor and 'the acted upon' across the undogmatic epiphenomenalism of holistic reductionism. The work, totally unmediated by structure, reason, style – or ability – became the material expression the fractally recursive noumena - simultaneously probabilistic in its creation and deterministic in its conception. He is most famously remembered by the circles he now frequents in Berlin for the maxim 'context is king, and you're a cunt.'

Clinical, Brutal....

Stewart Home was born in south London in 1962. He developed an interest in northern soul and punk rock as a teenager, and from 1974 onwards spent a lot of his time hanging around the West End of London, both alone and in the company of other juveniles.

After leaving school at the age of sixteen, he first signed on the dole in the late seventies, and last claimed unemployment benefits in the mid-nineties. He has never held down a regular job for more than a few months at a time. On those rare occasions when he's been forced to work, Home has taken employment as a factory labourer, agricultural labourer, shop assistant, office clerk and art class model.

Deciding he didn't like working in factories as a teenager, Home pursued cultural and political interests, writing many books and participating in even more gallery exhibitions. He lives in London. Thames water, rather than blood, is said to run through Home's veins.

A.D. Hitchin is a poetry and prose writer published extensively in small press and independent journals including *Blaze VOX*, *Dogmatika* and *3:AM*. You can catch newly updated work at: www.myspace.com/antonyhitchin

Richard Kovitch is a Writer / Producer / Director who lives in Central London. He has been published by *3:AM Magazine*, *Dogmatika* and *Black Listed Thoughts* while his work for television has won awards in the UK, Europe and the United States. He is currently developing a series of film projects and blogs regularly at The Drift – http://richardkovitch-thedrift.blogspot.com/.

Lee Kwo: I have been writing for forty years/ Ten Novels and 3 books of poetry/ Traveled thru Europe and Asia in 1974 as Lee Beckworth/ Disappeared from Paris and was never heard of again/ Turned up ten yrs later in Sydney as the Avatar Lee Kwo/Supported my self as a musician/bass and sax/ Influences from Pharaoh Sanders to Weather Report/ and from 1980 original material/ Influenced by Japanese Noise Music/ Currently publishing first Novel A Celibate Autopsy/The first Post Human Novel/Based on the premis that another consciousness will take over the human paradigm of affectation/the processing of information as pure desire at speed way beyond human capacity/ Transgressing the limits of the flesh and interpretation of the void left by the death of god/ I attempt to document within the limts of the imaginary metaphors of a bankrupt language/the next singularity/an evolutionary step which may not be the paradigm of human consciousness as we know it/ This task takes the word as Machinic at velocity past the cyberpunk works of such literary idols as Kenji Siratori which still maintans a humanist presence/ In my work I aspire to the post digital forming strange new becomings/ word becomes noise again / This is not Science Fiction this is Bizarre Device/ The annihilation of the human as species by its own obsession with the limits of violence and pornography/

Jim Lopez was born and raised in Los Angeles. He has a Masters Degree from Harvard Divinity School, Harvard University. He writes a column titled "The Last Dregs of Poverty" for *Paraphilia Magazine*, and his writings have appeared in *Exquisite Corpse*, *Brutarian Magazine*, the *Pasadena Weekly* and the *Dudley Review: Literary Magazine*. 'Rubber-Hose Real Estate' is from his collection of short stories in his

Clinical, Brutal....

forthcoming book *Abstracts of An American Pageant: Reality Principle of an Aphasic Metempsychosis*, to be published by Paraphilia Books.

Díre McCain is a five-dimensional creature who fell through a Lorentzian traversable wormhole into a three-dimensional universe, landing on what was, at the time, the second rock from the Sun. After a nebulous sojourn in the Zone of Avoidance, while trapped in a self-induced state of suspended animation, she was unwittingly converted into a transportable energy pattern, and ultimately rematerialized on twenty-first century Earth. "Suffers from" Aboulomania, Planomania, Eleutheromania, Habromania, Hydrodipsomania, a severe case of Logomania, and innocuous Daddy Issues. Possesses a ridiculous number of utterly useless skills, including the mythical mantic Seventh Sense, which is merely another of myriad delusional beliefs. Subsists on sincerity, empathy, tolerance, love, and Skippy Natural Super Chunk Peanut Butter. Can be found loitering at www.diremccain.com and www.paraphiliamagazine.com.

D M Mitchell is the author of *A Serious Life*, being a history of Savoy Books in the context of the underground literary scene in particular the period from 1960 and 2004. He has edited and contributed to two anthologies inspired by H P Lovecraft (*The Starry Wisdom* and *Songs of the Black Wurm Gism*) published by Creation Books. His essays, stories, introductions and other material have appeared in numerous publications in Europe and America. He is currently co-editing *Paraphilia Magazine* with Dire McCain (www.paraphiliamagazine.com) and has two books forthcoming from Paraphilia Books.

He lives in Wales.

Christopher Nosnibor is a writing machine. He's also a music obsessive, and combines these elements of his life in the copious reviews he produces for Whisperin' and Hollerin.' He also has an endless capacity for churning out high-octane fiction, social commentary and general spouting. He has had short stories published in numerous zines, which include *Neonbeam*, *The Toronto Quarterly* and *Paraphilia Magazine*, and has a handful of longer works in print, including *THE PLAGIARIST* and *Postmodern Fragments: Writings on Work, Technology and Contemporary Living*, both published by Clinicality Press. He has appeared as a featured author on the BBC website. He likes real ale and single malt whiskies.

Simon Phillips is an obscure web-poet who in 2003 managed to be one of the chosen poets to deliver his own 'Weapons of Mass Destruction Blues' poem along with 10,000 other poems to 10 Downing St. on behalf of Poets Against The War. He was a consultant and participant in Beatrice Gibson's reworking of Cornelius Cardew's 'The Great Learning' at www.thegreatlearning.org. In an earlier life he was onstage dancer and general idiot for the failed 90's rock act Mansworth / Ice Mummies, an experience that he sort of re-told in his long unpublished novel Going Nowhere Fast. Since the late 80's he has been the London member of Chicago's Unofficial Soup Kitchen where as his alter ego Bejesus he now runs the www.usk.org in a very quiet corner of the web!

Lucius Rofocale was raised in the wilderness by wolves and although 'rescued' and indoctrinated as a Homo-sapien, remains very feral. He can be reached at luciusrofocale@live.com.

Clinical, Brutal....

Constance Stadler has been writing, publishing, and editing poetry from the 'prehistoric' epoch of print journals to modern e-times. She was a former editor of *South and West* and is currently a contributing editor to the e-zine *Eviscerator Heaven* and Review Editor for *Calliope Nerve*. She has published over 300 poems and three chapbooks in her 'first manifestation' as a poet, and has just released her first two chaps in 20 years, *Tinted Steam* (Shadow Archer Press) *Sublunary Curse* (Erbacce) and an eBook, *Paper Cuts* (Calliope Nerve).

Her most recent work appears in such 'zines *as BlazeVox, ditch, ken*again, Pen Himalaya, Rain Over Bouville, Clockwise Cat, Unlikely Stories 2.0, Hanging Moss, Neonbeam,* and *Gloom Cupboard.* She has been recently 'Featured Poet' for the *Guild of Outsider Writers, Counterexample Poetics* and *The Poetry Warrior*.

Bill Thunder is the real deal. He's one seriously hard-boiled motherfucker. He's the bastardizer. Credited with devising the move known as 'the full cuntal lobotomy' as a method of interrogation, it's wise not to fuck with him. A PI by day and also by night, he recently turned his hand to writing. *THE BASTARDIZER* (2009) is his first novel, and is published by Clinicality Press.

pablo vision is a multimedia artist. There are several published stories *about* him. His artwork (dis)graces the covers of other writers' books and burns retinas online.

Information about current projects and links to his work – including audio, film, and reviews – can be found at http://pablovision.blogspot.com/ and his virtual office space at Epic Rites Press can be located at http://www.epicrites.org/

Also published by Clinicality Press

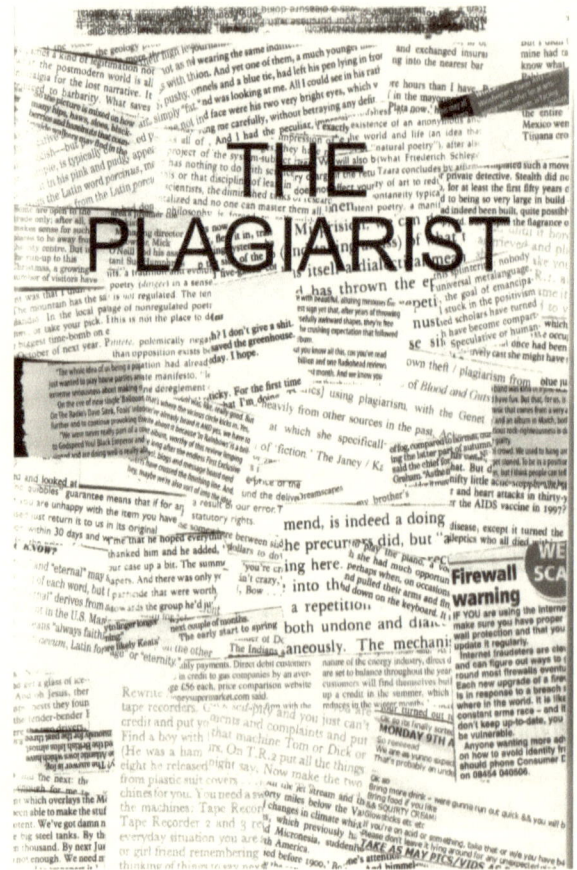

THE PLAGIARIST by Christopher Nosnibor.

199 pages, US Trade. The definitive anti-novel, described as 'like the work of William Burroughs on steroids.' Available as hardback with dust jacket exclusively from Clinicality Press priced £10.99, and trade paperback via Clinicality and all good on-line retail channels, rrp. £7.50.

Also published by Clinicality Press

Postmodern Fragments: Writings on Work, Technology and Contemporary Living by Christopher Nosnibor.

42 pages, US Trade paperback. A collection of essays and short works of fiction which share the common theme of life in the (post)modern society. Available as a trade paperback via Clinicality and all good on-line retail channels, rrp. £4.99.

Clinical, Brutal....

Also published by Clinicality Press

The Bastardizer by Bill Thunder.

187 pages. An ultra-hardboiled detective novel: it's abrasive, violent and action-packed. Will Thunder find Michael Jackson? Available as a Clinicality Press Pocket Edition, exclusively from Clinicality Press priced £4.99.

Coming soon as a trade paperback via Clinicality and all good on-line retail channels.